GW00738684

Josephine Pullein-Thompson has been involved with horses all her life. She opened a Riding School with her sisters when she was fifteen. She started writing at sixteen and published her first book, It Began with Picotee, with her sisters Diana and Christine. Their mother Joanna Cannan also wrote books. She might be said to have invented the genre of pony books when she wrote A Pony For Jean in 1936. Josephine Pullein-Thompson has published forty books for children. She is now President of the PEN Club in London and was made an MBE in 1984. This book was inspired by a visit to a racing stables, where Josephine rode exercised and acted as a pace setter on the gallops.

# RACE HORSE
# HOLIDAY

**Josephine Pullein-Thompson**

**CAVALIER PAPERBACKS**

© Josephine Pullein-Thomspon 1971

Reprinted by Cavalier Paperbacks 1996

Burnham House
Jarvis Street
Upavon
Wilts SN9 6DU

This books is sold subject to the condition that it shall
not, by way of trade or otherwise, be lent, re-sold, hired
out or otherwise circulated without the publisher's prior
consent in any form of binding or cover other than that in
which it is published and without a similar condition
including this condition being imposed on the subsequent
purchaser.

ISBN 1-899470-11-5

Printed and bound by Cox and Wyman, Reading, Berks

# CHAPTER ONE

## OFF TO EASTCOMBE

"I DO hope that nothing will go wrong," said my mother looking down at her half-packed suitcase. "Alex says that it will be nice for Angela to have your company, but I don't know—last time I saw her she seemed so grown-up for her age. Don't let her lead you astray, Vivien, and don't let Jon leap on any half-broken racehorses. We shall be such miles away. I wish now that I'd never agreed to go. I feel so guilty going off and leaving the pair of you for three whole weeks, but I've always longed to travel and this did seem a chance in a thousand."

I said, "There's no need to feel guilty. Think of all that invigorating fresh air blowing off the downs, it'll be much better for us than the polluted atmosphere of Marsden, and if Angela's too old for me there's still Katie."

Mummy giggled. "Katie's eight. And I *still* feel guilty," she insisted as she packed a large double photograph frame holding portraits of Jon and I aged nine and ten.

"You can't take that," I objected, "it'll make you pounds overweight."

"I don't care, I'm going to take it whatever else I have to leave behind," Mummy answered obstinately.

As Mummy said, this trip to Russia was a chance in

a thousand. Daddy's firm, battling for exports, had landed a contract for a whole machine-tool factory and he was going out on the engineering side to help set it up. He expected to be there for three or four months and when the firm had offered a three week trip for wives, Mummy had decided that it would be easier to send us away in the holidays than to arrange for someone to live with us during the term.

Other people seem to have masses of useful grandparents and aunts with whom they stay when their parents want to rush off somewhere, but Mummy was an only child and at this moment her father was ill and her mother very busy looking after him. Daddy has only one brother who lives in Australia and *his* parents had gone out there on a long visit. But, though we don't have many relations, Mummy and Daddy are very good at producing old friends. Alex Grant, the racehorse trainer, had lived on the next farm to Daddy when they were boys, gone to the same schools and been best man at our parents' wedding; it was at his racing stable that we were to spend the next three weeks.

Though we assured them that we were perfectly capable of travelling on our own, Mummy and Daddy insisted that they must see us on to the train for Longbridge before they set off on their own journey. This infuriated Jon who loves airports and had planned to see *them* off and it meant that we all went up to London together and whizzed about expensively in taxis with our parents looking unfamiliarly elegant in their new clothes.

I had been looking forward to our stay at Eastcombe stables, but, as the train bore us out of the

6

station and the waving figures were lost to view, I became very gloomy. Angela Grant, two years older *and* old for her age, would certainly despise me. We hadn't seen Alex Grant for three years; supposing both Jon and I became tongue-tied and quite unable to think of things to say. Our clothes were probably wrong for a racing stable and our riding, though considered passable on Marsden Common, would appear disgracefully amateur in real horsy circles.

Then Jon spoke. "I wonder what it feels like to watch your father blast off into space," he said delving in the knapsack. "Are you ready for a sausage roll yet? I'm starving."

After a sausage roll, a hardboiled egg, a bag of crisps and some chocolate I felt less gloomy. I reminded myself that I'd always wished that we lived a more adventurous life instead of being just an ordinary English family in a pleasant London suburb. Marsden has trees and gardens and the Common; three riding schools, two cinemas and an ice-skating rink, but it's not the sort of place where you expect adventure. We'd lived a dull, safe, orderly life: Daddy going to work, us to school, Mummy coping with the house and the shopping. In the holidays we'd ridden once a week, or more if our grandparents gave us money for birthdays, at Jean Morris's riding school, which we liked best as you were allowed to help with the grooming and tack cleaning and sometimes even asked to fetch ponies from fields, which meant bare-back rides across the Common.

Alex Grant was the sort of person who had adventures. He'd ridden in the Grand National when he was nineteen, farmed in Canada, worked in stables in

7

France and then deciding to train, had become assist-
ant to a famous trainer to learn the job, or so Daddy
had said, before he opened his own stables. Then
there was the mystery of Mrs Grant. Our parents had
warned us that we were not to mention her as she had
eloped with her husband's richest owner and now
lived in great luxury in London and Sardinia. The
absence of a mother was what really worried Mummy
when she fussed over Angela leading me astray and
though Daddy had pointed out that we would be in
the depths of the country and surrounded by what he
called 'motherly women' like the Head Lad's wife, and
that Alex himself was the father of two daughters, I
knew that Mummy had continued to worry in silence.
I, on the other hand, had longed all my life for older
brothers and sisters or even cousins who would suggest mad and lovely things to do and whirl me along
with them into every sort of adventure. I quite like
Jon, but younger brothers are not much use. You have
to drag them along with you, stir them up into doing
things and even when they grow and suddenly begin
to tower above you, they're hopeless at life and still
want you to do the asking and even if you give them
the money to pay in coffee bars they always drop it or
something.

It was Angela who met us at the station. Her long
hair, gold and wavy, was loose and she wore crumpled
jeans and a long droopy purple waistcoat over a pink
shirt. Beads and chains and bracelets clanked about
her. Her fingers were embellished with four huge rings,
her eyes hidden by a pair of enormous dark glasses. I
felt suddenly furious that Mummy had made me travel
in a very dull blue skirt that was too tight anyway.

8

Behind Angela stood a tiny man with bowed legs, wearing riding clothes and a cap. For a terrible moment I thought it was Alex Grant shrunk but then I realised that he was too old.

"This is Bert Langton, the yard-man," said Angela as he seized my suitcase. We said, "How do you do?" and followed them to an estate car parked outside.

Angela said, "I haven't passed my driving test yet, so Bert has to sit beside me. He's terrified."

"And that's the truth," agreed Bert, buckling his seat belt.

Eastcombe was nine miles from Longbridge and the drive was quite exciting, especially when we reached the downs; huge bare humps, grey-green and elephantine in the pale spring sun. It was also quite frightening. Bert's nervousness communicated itself to me and I couldn't help noticing that Angela was inclined to take corners on the wrong side of the road. I was quite glad when, in the midst of the downs, we came to Eastcombe. You could only enter it by going steeply downhill, only leave it by climbing steeply up. The village was small, just a few cottages clustered together and beyond it there was a sharp turn in the road, a huge notice demanding "Slow—Racehorses", and then an uphill drive with post and rail fences on either side and a horse or two in very tidy paddocks. "That chestnut's Sporting Print, he was a real good horse, ran well as a two-year old—then broke down at Sandown," Bert started, and then broke off to cry, "*Steady*, Angela, mind that gatepost!" But we'd already swept through with a slight scraping noise and were drawing up with a flourish in front of a long white house.

It was a plain, almost severe-looking house. The walls were very white, the door and large sash windows newly painted black, but there were no roses or creepers climbing up it and no flower beds in front, only well-raked gravel. Some people's houses are very important to them but somehow when you looked at the Grants' you knew that it wasn't; you could see that it was really just a place to live and that what really mattered lay beyond, at the end of the drive, where, through a pair of impressive pillars, we could see a large, square stable yard.

Bert said, "I expect you'll want to see the horses first. The lads'll be opening up for evening stables in ten minutes or a quarter of an hour."

"No they don't," Angela interrupted him bluntly. "They want to see the house and have tea. They'll have more than enough of those beastly horses in the next three weeks."

"What a way for a trainer's daughter to talk," said Bert, handing out suitcases.

Feeling rather cheated, because, of course, I was longing to see the stables, I followed Angela into the house.

"Leave your luggage here," she said, "and I'll show you downstairs first."

The dining-room and drawing-room were very grand, but at the back of the house there was a much nicer sitting-room with television and books and a general mess of toys and dressmaking.

"We have to keep some rooms tidy for the owners," Angela explained. "They're inclined to turn up unexpectedly to see their beastly nags and they have to be properly entertained—sat down in the drawing-room

10

and given whisky, not instant coffee in the kitchen like everyone else."

The kitchen was at the back of the house between the sitting-room and the office, which had its own outside door so that you could reach the stables without going through the rest of the house. The office was the really horsy room; there was a huge desk piled with papers and a filing cabinet, but the walls were entirely covered with photographs and paintings and sketches of horses, except for a few shelves which held crowded ranks of tarnished silver cups.

Then we went upstairs. There the arrangement was rather like a stable-yard—a corridor running along the back of the house with all the bedrooms on the same side opening off it and a bathroom at either end. Katie and Angela had rooms on either side of the stairs, mine was next to Angela's and Jon had the one beyond at the end of the house next to the stables.

They were nice rooms with views of the downs, and of the stables if you put your head out of the window. Then Angela showed us her room. It had crimson curtains, a deep purple divan cover, a white rug and was in· a state of total confusion. There were clothes and shoes everywhere mixed up with books and magazines, tennis rackets, riding boots and dirty coffee mugs. I privately imagined Mummy's horror, considering the fuss she makes over one banana skin under the bed, but it made me like Angela better; somehow she seemed more human, less grown-up. She took us down to the huge kitchen. There was an Aga cooker at one end against which sat a fox-terrier called Rom and two tabby cats, all warming their backs.

"I'll show you where everything lives," said Angela,

"then you can help yourselves whenever you feel hungry. That's what we do. We have proper lunch because Mrs Hinde comes up from the village to cook it, but otherwise we fry bacon and eggs or sausages or fish fingers or make coffee and toast for ourselves whenever we need it."

She took us on a conducted tour of the larder, the refrigerator and the kitchen cupboards and then she put the kettle on. "Katie'll be in any moment—she's gone for a ride with two of the apprentices. Can you see the teabags, Vivien? They should be in the cupboard by your head. Here Jon, can you start making toast?" By the time I'd put teabags into pottery mugs and Angela had dumped butter, jam and milk on the kitchen table, there was a clatter outside and Katie came in through the back door. She was very like Angela—a much smaller edition, of course, but she had the same wavy gold hair, only hers was tied in a pony tail, the same wide face, brown eyes and strong dark eyebrows.

I can never get over other families matching. Jon and I have come out so different; he with crisp chestnut-brown hair and brown eyes and a withdrawn expression, while I have dead straight, pitch-black hair and dark blue eyes and a small face.

Katie was saying "Hullo" when another face came round the door, it was a boy's face. He said, "She rolled off. I don't think she hurt herself. Pincushion swerved."

"Of course I didn't hurt myself," said Katie going to the door and dragging at his arm. "I'd have cried if I had. *Do* come in, Mark, *please*."

The boy muttered something and Katie turned to her sister.

"It's not true that you don't want him coming in any more because you're on Geoff's side, is it?" she asked.

"No, of course it's not. I'm not going to take sides in their silly squabble, life's too short," said Angela. "If Mark wants tea it's here as usual."

The boy came in. He was very thin, about two inches shorter than me and walked with a slight limp. His hair was dark brown and straight, his eyes blue and I liked the look of his thin, bony face.

"Where's Jim?" asked Katie.

"Gone to start his mucking out," Mark answered. "He's slow, takes twice as long as anyone else to do his two. Mr Phelps gets enraged when he's not ready to feed with everyone else."

"Oh, Vivien and Jon Bradley," Angela introduced us. She'd made her tea and Katie's and the rest of us made our own. Jon produced a huge pile of toast.

"How did Goldie go?" asked Angela.

"A bit scatty," Mark answered, "especially when Jim couldn't stop Chunky and Katie came off. I wish he'd get it into his head that you *can* walk and trot on grass."

"I like him lively. I love fast horses, do you?" Angela asked me.

I said "Yes," firmly though I felt a quake of terror go through me as I saw myself hurtling at supersonic speed up a racecourse on an enormous and unstoppable horse.

Jon was asking Mark questions about racehorses but Mark, with one eye on the clock, was trying to

13

eat his toast and drink his tea and could only give brief answers. "Must go," he said as he downed his last mouthful. Katie was much more talkative. She told us all about Jim, the newest apprentice, who was, she said, very, very nervous. "Mark says when he goes out with the string he's frightened out of his wits. He's got two of the quietest horses to ride—Steel and Old Rosie—but he's so frightened he hangs on to them and they get fidgety and upset and Dad yells at him. That's why Mark's teaching him on Chunky."

When we'd finished tea Katie said she'd show us Pincushion and the ponies we were to ride. We followed her out of the back door over to some loose boxes behind the house, quite separate from the main stable yard. Pincushion had a special low door so that he could see out. He was tiny and completely round, all his outlines were curved, but he wasn't hairy, in fact he had rather an elegant mane and tail and large, toad-like eyes. He was a peculiar colour, not bay or brown or liver chestnut or dun but a mixture of all of them, well stirred. Jon said that there would have to be a new official colour "Mud", but Katie told us with pride that he was mouse dun and most unusual.

Then we inspected Angela's Crock of Gold, a very well-bred looking golden chestnut, and Chunky, a liver chestnut cob with a white blaze.

"You're to ride him, Jon," Katie told us. "He's really the trainer's cob, but Dad always goes up to the gallops in the Land-Rover nowadays and so the apprentices learn on Chunky. He's a boy's horse, Dad says, so we borrowed a pony for Vivien. She's out in the paddock because she lives out at home."

14

I was rather dismayed when I saw the shaggy skew-bald. She looked so disreputable after the Grant ponies. Not that they were clipped but they had the thin clean coats of horses which have been stabled all winter, and beautifully pulled manes and tails. "She's called Princess Amelia," said Katie. "She's awfully dirty." We talked to the unprincess-like pony for a bit. At least she had a nice nature, I told myself, squashing down my disappointment and trying not to feel hard done by; at least I had no need to dread supersonic speeds on a huge unstoppable horse, for the Princess was much more disreputable and unfit than the Marsden Common ponies and she looked about 14.2, the size I was used to.

Katie said, "Well, now I'm going to watch television. You can come if you like, but it might be a bit young for you; it's too young for Angela."

"What about the racehorses?" asked Jon. "Would it be all right if we went and looked at them?"

"Yes, no one will mind, but you mustn't get in the way," Katie answered and ran off towards the house.

"Do you suppose that means it's really all right?" asked Jon.

"Well, we might as well go and have a quick look," I said, "and if Mark's about we can ask him." I was dying to see the racehorses. I couldn't understand the Grants lack of interest at all.

The big yard was full of bustle. Mucking out and grooming, unrugging and rugging up all seemed to be going on at once and the horses were mostly tied up. There were twenty-two loose boxes, sixteen of them were occupied and two others looked ready for their occupants' return. The stables were brick built

*"The big yard was full of bustle."*

16

with blue-painted doors and windows; at the far end they were two-storied and you could see that people lived above. In the middle of this side there was an archway leading into another little yard and above the arch was a large clock. A circle of turf, protected by white posts and chains, in the centre of the yard and the tubs of daffodils scattered round it made it the most elegant horse establishment I had ever seen.

We looked round for Mark and found him, with his coat off and his sleeves rolled up, grooming a dapple grey with great energy.

"This is Moonstruck," he said when he saw us at the door. "She's a good class filly—three-year-old. We haven't had her long. She was trained by Mat Codling last season but he and her owner Mr Sinclair bust up over something. Bit of luck for Eastcombe—she won almost every time out as a two-year-old."

"She looks lovely," I said.

"Bit long and low, bit heavy on the shoulder," answered Mark critically. "For looks I'd rather have my other one, High Jester, bay colt on your left. Two-year-old, untried. He's a lovely ride."

We looked at High Jester, who, groomed, rugged, watered and hayed up, looked ready for the night. He had a finer head than Moonstruck, it was beautifully shaped, clear cut and already wise-looking; he was bay with black points and a white star. We couldn't see the rest of him because of his rug.

I went back to Moonstruck's door and said, "I can see what you mean." And Jon asked, "Is it all right for us to walk round or shall we be in the way?"

"Be o.k. if you don't hold the lads up by asking too many questions," answered Mark. "And if you go in a box mind you pick your feet up as you come out. Nothing infuriates Mr Phelps more than visitors who drag half the bedding out on their feet."

Jon said, "Right," and I decided that I wouldn't enter a loose box or speak a word.

Next to Mark was a reddish-haired boy with a tiny mouth and a very pointed chin and beyond him an older, almost grown-up lad with wide shoulders and dark curly hair. Beyond him, I was surprised to see two girls, who looked about twenty and were talking to each other non-stop as they rushed in and out with haynets and rugs.

I began to feel rather out of place, knowing no one and having nothing to do. "Let's go back to the house," I suggested to Jon. "We've got to unpack and if Angela's still wearing jeans I'll put mine on."

# CHAPTER TWO

### HIGH JESTER

I WAKENED early with the light greyish and inhospitable at my window, I lay listening to the whinnies, the clank of buckets and the voices from the stable yard. When I prised open my eyes enough to see my watch, I found it was a quarter to seven. There had been no suggestion that we should ride out on exercise with the racehorses. I felt glad and sorry about it at the same time; glad that we wouldn't have to expose our Marsden Common riding before the experts, sorry not to have the marvellous experience. Still, there were three weeks, I reminded myself.

Alex Grant had come home about half past nine the night before, rather gloomy from an unsuccessful day at the races. He'd found Angela and us lolling before the television—and after he'd asked if we had everything we wanted, and whether we had had enough to eat, he told Angela to look after us and take us for a ride over the downs. Then he said that it was time we all went to bed.

Angela had been indignant at this and said she wasn't a child. "Well, please yourselves," her father had told her, "but as I have to be up at six-thirty I'm off as soon as I've walked round the stables and locked up."

I had felt rather awkward. It's difficult being a guest when your hosts disagree with each other. I'd waited for a bit and then said I felt sleepy and Jon said he did too, so we'd left Angela dressmaking defiantly and gone to bed.

Alex Grant, I thought, didn't look much like a racehorse trainer. Well, not my idea of a trainer anyway. Except for his tweedy suit and healthy outdoor look he could have been in advertising or something. He wasn't weatherbeaten enough nor did he have faded blue eyes which gazed into the distance. His eyes were brown like his daughters' and his dark hair was cut in a modern style. I wondered whether he minded Angela being so unhorsy and wondering I must have fallen asleep. I woke again to the scrunch of hoofs on gravel and the light at the window yellow with sunshine. I leapt out of bed and rushed to look out. A long string of horses was walking down the drive. They looked lovely with their coats glistening in the sunlight and their riders perched on top, all riding with incredibly short stirrups. I left the window and rushed into Jon's room. "You must look, quickly," I said, pulling back his curtains. "The horses are going out."

Jon groaned, muttered angrily and then dragged himself out of bed, but by the time he joined me we could only see the tail end of the string disappearing down the drive and Alex Grant, in a sheepskin coat and cavalry twill trousers, climbing into his Land-Rover to follow.

"Waking me up, practically giving me a heart attack, just for that," grumbled Jon as he scurried back to bed. I couldn't go back to bed, having seen the horses. It seemed a terrible waste to lie there when we could be out riding on the downs. Even the disreputable Princess Amelia seemed alluring now that the sun was shining.

"Aren't you longing to try Chunky?" I asked Jon. "Angela said we were to do exactly what we liked. We could have breakfast and then go for a ride."

"Or we could stay in bed," mumbled Jon.

"But it's ten minutes to nine," I protested, "and a fine day; there may not be another for weeks. *Do* get up, Jon."

He only groaned so I went back to my room, dressed in jodhpurs and sweater, and after listening at Angela's door and hearing only steady breathing, crept downstairs.

It was rather fun getting one's breakfast in a strange kitchen. I had orange juice—there was a jug in the refrigerator—and I had started making toast and coffee when, to my surprise, Jon appeared also wearing jodhpurs.

"Let's have scrambled eggs," he said. "I'll make them." We ate our huge breakfast and there was still no sign of the Grants so we washed up and then went out to the stables behind the house. Princess Amelia had been brought in and stood in a box next to Chunky and in the box, making a loud hissing noise as he groomed, was Bert. "I'm glad *someone* intends to ride. I was beginning to think that we'd got another Angela come to stay. 'Ere," he handed me a dandy brush, "I've knocked the worst off her and cut a foot off her tail. Her mane needs pulling but that'll 'ave to wait till one of the girls has a minute to spare. Princess Amelia!" he laughed scornfully. "Proper Robinson Crusoe, that's what she looks."

I started work and from the stable door Jon asked, "Can I have something to groom Chunky with and will you show us their tack?"

Organized and aided by Bert we were soon ready. He gave me instructions about cleaning the Princess's cardboard-stiff tack after the ride and taught Jon how to put on a running martingale. He told us the way to the downs and instructed us to keep well away from the racehorses, especially since the Princess was a stranger and a mare. "And don't go careering about on the gallops or you'll get the rough side of Mr Grant's tongue," he called after us as we set off.

What with Mr Phelps' reign of terror in the stables and Alex Grant's rough tongue on the downs, I was beginning to feel distinctly nervous. So when we came round the corner of the house and met the string returning up the drive I turned and fled back to our stables. Jon followed me, protesting "Why did you tear off like that? There was plenty of room. I wanted to see them go past," he grumbled.

"Amelia's a sort of leper," I answered, "and if you'd got up a bit faster this morning you'd have seen them then."

We waited until we felt sure they would all be in the yard before we emerged again. Then we rode down the drive and to the sharp corner just before the village where the track led up to the downs. As we climbed up the wet, chalky track my spirits rose. It was wonderful to be riding towards great areas of unknown countryside, and to be our own masters. I loved riding at Marsden but there was a certain sameness about it; this was a real adventure. The hill grew steeper, Princess Amelia began to puff and I called to Jon, who was riding on ahead on the fit Chunky, to wait. But when he reached the top and the track widened and became hedgeless, allowing the wind to buffet us and views to appear in every direction, the Princess became more lively. Because she looked so disreputable I'd expected her to be unschooled and a dreary ride, but I quickly found that she wasn't. As soon as she trotted I realised that she had a long, low stride and when we cantered, setting off recklessly into the immense distance before us, I recognised how well-trained, how willing and yet how controllable she was. I began to enjoy myself more and more.

A notice asked people to keep off the gallops but there was plenty of track beside the green mowed and rolled strip. As we galloped I felt like singing. Jon was still ahead and presently feeling Amelia tire, I called to him to slow up. When we were walking side by side, both patting our horses enthusiastically, I asked him what Chunky was like.

"He's a bit rough," Jon answered. "He sort of pounds along, but he's really keen; I like him." As I described the Princess's unexpected abilities I realised that I had ceased to feel hard done by. I didn't envy Jon Chunky at all; I'd rather skim than pound.

We walked until the Princess began to suggest another canter and then we sped on to the very end of the down where a wire fence funnelled us into a narrow track leading downhill. We stopped and looked about us. The track led to a cultivated valley; we could see a farm and a road between us and the next great down, which rose steeply and imposingly from tame-looking fields. On our left was a hunting gate and we could see a grassy path leading to a small round hill. "Shall we go down there?" I suggested, tempted by the springy look of the bright green turf.

"Yes, why not?" agreed Jon. "I don't suppose any one wants us back until lunchtime. We could ride to the top of that little hill."

Directly we were below the skyline the wind ceased to buffet us and we had to lower our voices which had grown used to shouting against it. When we reached the foot of the down we had an exciting canter over the hillocky turf. There were so many ups and downs that you got a wonderful switchback effect that was much more fun than cantering on level ground.

On the top of the round hill we dismounted and let the ponies graze.

"I wish I knew their names," I said, looking at the downs which crowded round us in a mountainous green sea.

"That one's got a fort on top of it," said Jon pointing. "We must go up there some time. I wonder if the Grants have a map."

Turning for Eastcombe we rode quietly up the path to the gallops and there, with the roar of the wind exciting the ponies again, we set off at a brisk canter. We were riding side by side enjoying ourselves enormously when we saw a lone horse coming towards us at a tremendous speed. We both stopped at once.

"Absolutely flat out," yelled Jon above the wind.

"Someone's fallen off. He's riderless," I shouted back, staring hard to make sure there was no tiny figure crouched over the withers.

"We'd better try to catch him," said Jon riding towards the forbidden gallops. But we could both see it was hopeless; the loose horse was going too fast to stop. If one succeeded in barring his way there would be a collision. The only thing to do was to go with him and hope that he would slow up gradually. We turned, looking back over our shoulders at the racehorse, who gained on us rapidly. Suddenly he gave a loud, frantic whinny. He was still going terribly fast. Ahead the gallops ended; there was the wire fence and the narrow track. I could just see him crashing into the fence.

"Down the track?" I shouted at Jon.

"I should think so," he answered, "but not at this pace; let's slow up a bit."

We reduced the speed of our canter and the bay

horse, stirrups, reins and the rug over his quarters flapping, was quickly upon us. He had slowed up too, but the three of us entered the narrow rutted track at a nerve-racking speed. Giving soothing cries of "Whoa" Jon and I rode on, looking apprehensively at the large, lurching young horse who careered behind us. At least he hadn't crashed into the wire fences. I slowed up Amelia and hoped that he wouldn't tread on her heels, that she wouldn't kick him and break his leg. We trotted, fast at first and then slower and slower until at last we were walking and both stretching out hands to grab the racehorse's rein. We came to a crowded halt. The young horse was dark with sweat and trembling all over; he put his nose to Chunky's and Amelia's in turn, asking for comfort. We let them talk for a bit and then, remembering Bert's words about Amelia being a stranger and a mare we decided that Jon should lead the colt. We crossed his stirrups and then set off up the track, Amelia and I following behind. When I saw that the young horse was going to lead I began to wonder whether he was a Grant horse and suddenly I recognised him. "Jon, has he got a star?" I shouted. "Is it High Jester?"

Jon peered at the racehorse. "Yes, I think he is," he answered. "He's certainly got a star, but he's so sweaty I'm not sure about his colour."

However, when we reached the top of the track all doubts were dispelled; we saw the Land-Rover rushing to meet us, Mark sitting in front beside Alex Grant. They both jumped out and without a word inspected High Jester. Alex ran his hand down each leg. Mark took the reins from Jon.

"He *seems* o.k.," said Alex in tones of disbelief.

"My God, what a piece of luck." He looked at us. "Where did you catch him?" We explained and then legging Mark up he said, *Walk* back with him to the other horses, will you? And walk slowly—he's only a two-year-old." He watched us anxiously as we set off and then, getting into the Land-Rover, bumped past us.

"What happened? How did you come off?" asked Jon, tactless as usual.

Mark looked miserable. "Something startled him. I don't know what but I suspect Geoff belted him one on the sly. Anyway, Jester shot off and when he put in a couple of quick bucks that was the end of me. I'm really in Mr Grant's black book now."

"But why?" I asked indignantly. "No one can help falling off, especially if Geoff really gave him one from behind."

"Coming off doesn't matter," Mark answered. "You could come off twenty times a day and bother no one; it's letting go of a horse, especially up here. You're supposed to hang on until you're trampled to death."

"Why would Geoff belt him one?" asked Jon.

"Jealous, I suppose," Mark answered. He suddenly smiled. "You see I had a bit of luck this morning. It seems that there's been a muddle over the jockey retained to ride Moonstruck on Saturday. He thought with the change of stables it was off and Mr. Sinclair, the owner, thought it was still fixed up. Anyway Mr Sinclair said it was too late to get anyone really good and he'd like me to have the ride. Mr Grant's a bit doubtful, but he's willing to let me have a go and Geoff's furious."

"Have you ridden in a race before?" I asked.

"Oh yes, but I've still got my seven pound allowance. When you've ridden six winners it goes down to five pounds—I've had four so far."

"Four winners!" I said amazed.

"That's not many. I'm hoping to do a lot better this season. That's why Moonstruck is such a bit of luck— she's entered for some good class races, not the Oaks but some good races and, on last season's form, she stands a chance. I'm hoping we can put the stable back among the winners. It's time Mr Grant's run of bad luck ended."

"What sort of horse is High Jester?" asked Jon, "will he win good races?"

"He's running for the first time the week after next," Mark answered. "He's got a good turn of speed. We gave him a trial with a couple of good three-year-olds and he held his own, but you can't give two-year-olds a lot of fast work, or you have them lame with sore shins in no time."

"He looked fast enough," I said, "when he was loose just now."

We came to a group of horses waiting in the middle of the gallops with Mr Phelps in charge. Apparently the proceedings were held up because Mark was needed to ride Sandy's horse, Clean Bill, in his fast work. Everyone seemed on edge. Mr Phelps was cursing people for being slow and getting in his way and Geoff, the dark, curly-haired apprentice, was quarrelling with one of the girls. Jon and I looked at each other and decided, reluctantly, that we'd better not stay to watch; keeping well clear of the gallops, we rode home.

We were met at the stables by a furious Katie who said that she had especially wanted to ride with us, that she would have got up early if she'd known and that we must see her ride Pincushion. We did our best to pacify her by offering to watch her ride that afternoon, but she was going out to tea with a friend so that was no good. We put our ponies away, checked their water and rubbed them down, hoping that our stable management was adequate but feeling rather at sea since there was no Bert about to tell us what to do. Then Angela called from the back door to say that she was making coffee. Would we like some? "We would," said Jon, breaking into a run, "I hope there's some food about, too, I'm starving."

We found Mrs Hinde in the kitchen. She was large and grey-haired, but brisk rather than motherly. She said that Katie's face was dirty, that never in all her born days had she seen a bedroom like Angela's and that we were all spoiling our lunch by eating between meals. Jon and I told of our adventures and of catching High Jester but when I came to Mark's theory that Geoff had walloped the horse unexpectedly from behind, Angela interrupted me at once. "You don't want to believe everything Mark says about Geoff," she told us. "They just don't get on. Geoff's the senior apprentice; he's almost eighteen so naturally he expects to boss the others around a bit. Mark's a good rider, there's no doubt about that, and he's two stone lighter than Geoff which gives him an enormous advantage, but the bit of success he's had seems to have gone to his head and now the other apprentices can't stand him."

"Jimmy likes him," argued Kate, "so do I. I like him twenty times as much as I like Geoff or Brian or Sandy."

"That's only because they don't pay you any attention," Angela told her.

When lunch appeared I could see Mrs Hinde's point about not eating between meals; it was very substantial: roast beef, baked roly-poly pudding. Alex carved and sat at the end of the table reading papers like *Raceform* and the *Sporting Times*. Katie chattered ceaselessly and Angela became silent and gloomy. Weighed down by so much food I sank into a sluggish silence too, but Jon seemed to think it was his duty to make conversation: he encouraged Katie who got sillier and sillier, and then he began to ask Alex questions about racing. At first they were general questions about the length of races but gradually he came round to Eastcombe stables and began to ask about High Jester's chances and whether Moonstruck would win on Saturday. Alex stood it for a bit and then he said, "Look, Jon, you must never ask trainers questions about their horses' form. A trainer's first duty is to the owner and naturally the owner wants nice long odds when he backs his horse so we keep quiet about the good ones. You can't keep anything really secret, the lads all see how a horse goes and though they're supposed to keep their mouths shut they often don't and occasionally someone succumbs to a bribe, but the less said the better—especially by the trainer."

Poor Jon went red in the face and said he was sorry but Alex answered, "No need to be," and retired behind his papers.

Angela muttered angrily about hating betting even more than she hated those beastly horses and began to clear the table. We were glad to be able to get up and help her. When we'd stacked the dishwasher Angela said that she had to do the shopping as Mrs Hinde had made a huge list and if we liked we could come into Longbridge.

## CHAPTER THREE

### TROUBLE WITH MOONSTRUCK

ANGELA had found us a large-scale map so for our second ride the next day Jon and I decided to explore the Rings, the ancient fortification on Fallbourne Down. It was a dull and drizzling morning so there were no fantastic views but again there were miles of springy turf, endless canters and gallops so we enjoyed ourselves tremendously. This time we had offered to take Katie with us, but she'd already fixed a lesson with Mark for the afternoon and she said that we *must* watch her then.

At lunch we were in the best of spirits after our lovely ride but we had to dampen them down to fit in with the gloomy atmosphere of the house. Only Katie was cheerful and she inquired minutely into every illness and accident either of us had ever had. I was rather dull—she didn't think much of whooping cough, chicken pox, 'flu and a sprained ankle but Jon could add mumps and a greenstick fracture of his arm when he was seven and the removal of his appendix at twelve. Katie was delighted with his stories of hospital life, mostly invented I think, but when she demanded to see his scar we changed the subject by inventing gruesome operations and illnesses for her teddy bears and dolls. Jon described the removal of all sorts of odd bits like sweetbreads and spleens, while I invented dropsical diseases when they grew immensely fat or withering ones which reduced them to wraiths. We rather enjoyed ourselves and even Angela looked less gloomy, but when Katie asked if she could leave the table Alex answered, "Yes, the sooner the better. I've never heard a more repulsive conversation." As you can imagine Jon and I finished our rhubarb pie in embarrassed silence and then retreated to the saddle room, where we consoled ourselves with the thought that though Alex might find our conversation trying, nothing could be ruder than his habit of eating his meals behind the *Racing Gazette*.

It seemed that Jimmy was having a lesson too. He was a pale boy with hair so fair it was almost white, and pale eyelashes and weak-looking pale blue eyes. He appeared to be about eleven but he told us that he was nearly fifteen.

"Mark's just coming; he said to get saddled up," he informed Katie, who promptly began to wail for me to help her. When Mark appeared he looked very gloomy and hardly spoke so we guessed that something had gone wrong. We followed him and his pupils into the small paddock behind our stables and found some oil drums to sit on while we watched. Mark seemed a very good instructor. He had lots to teach and said many of the same things that Jean Morris says to us at our winter sessions in the covered school. Kate didn't ride very well. She chattered all the time

*"The Princess jumped beautifully, fast and with scope . . ."*

instead of attending but she seemed brave, which Jim certainly wasn't. He tried so hard that he was stiff with anxiety and he obviously hated cantering on Chunky.

When they began popping over tiny jumps I could bear it no longer and rushed to fetch Princess Amelia. Jon and I both rode her, the other one helped Mark build the course, which was very low and mostly made out of bundles of brushwood and poles on oil drums. The Princess jumped beautifully, fast and with scope and not straight up into the air like Chunky, who gave poor Jim some nasty moments. He was happier when Mark changed him on to Pincushion, who was running out with Katie. After he had jumped a clear round we stopped and took our horses in.

Jon and Katie and I decided to clean tack and Mark and Jimmy went off to fetch theirs to clean it with us. Of course it wasn't long before Jon asked the question I was longing to ask but had decided would be tactless. Without disguising it at all he asked baldly, "How did Moonstruck go?"

Mark stopped dismantling his saddle and looking very depressed he said, "Terrible, just terrible. I couldn't get any steam up at all. Middlemarch just galloped away from us; he's a useful horse, but nothing special. Mr Grant said the time was terrible, too."

Jon asked, "What do you think caused it? I mean, she's supposed to be fast, isn't she?"

Mark seemed quite pleased to talk it over. "She's always been idle in her work," he said, "but a lot of good horses are like that until you get them upsides with another and start racing. Mr Grant doesn't believe in a lot of fast work. He trains mostly at the half-speed canter and even then you've got to push her along, but, well, it never occurred to me that she wouldn't go on if I asked for it. I mean, she won some good races last season. I can't understand it."

"Geoff could have done something," suggested Jim.

"What could he have done?" I asked, remembering Angela's words.

"A bucket of water can slow a horse up," said Mark gloomily. "I suppose he *could* have given her one when we were doing the first lot. You see we feed and muck them all out and brush the first lot over before we go to breakfast. Then we take the first lot out, come back and groom them properly. After that we brush over the second lot and take them out. But I don't think he'd go that far, Jim."

"I do," said Jimmy "and Brian and Sandy are on his side; they wouldn't give him away."

"Of course horses that have done well as two-year-olds do sometimes go off form at three. Sometimes they're ridden too hard, a jockey gets his whip out and they never forget it and they won't try again. Mr Grant's going to telephone the owner and find out what sort of race she had last time out, so we may learn something."

"Just like this stable's luck," said Jim.

Tactfully for once, Jon changed the subject; he began to ask questions about an apprentice's life. Being wakened at six a.m. six days a week seemed to us a terrible fate; Mark said he'd got used to it and Jimmy said Mr Phelps looked in at 6.15 to make sure things were moving so you *had* to get up.

"And how long are you apprenticed for?" asked Jon.

"Until I'm twenty-one," Mark answered, "and I

hope by then to have made enough of a name for myself so that some stable will give me a retainer and the rest will all be queueing up to offer me rides when I'm free," he laughed.

"And if you don't make a name?" said Jon.

"You have to be a stable lad. That's also your fate if you become too heavy unless you go into a jumping stable and ride under National Hunt rules. Of course you can become a head lad or a travelling head, which wouldn't be a bad life."

"What about you, Jim?" asked Jon.

"I haven't finished my six months trial so I dunno yet whether Mr. Grant'll take me on," Jim answered.

"He will," Mark spoke with conviction. "For one thing you're *so* light you're just what he wants for the next batch of yearlings. Sandy, Brian and I broke the last lot, but they'll both be too heavy for the next lot so it'll be you and me."

"Do you really ride yearlings?" I asked rather horrified.

"Well, you see, you've got to get them started if they're going to race as two-year-olds," Mark explained. "You've got to have light boys to ride them and you don't do much with them: a bit of lungeing, walk and trot them round the cinder track, then riding figures of eight with an old horse beside them so that they learn to go upsides with another or a bit of cantering following the old horse."

"And then they race at two?" asked Jon.

"Yes, the end of March the season starts but the early races are all short ones, about five furlongs—just over half a mile. And, of course, they're fed specially to bring them on. When you buy them at the yearling sales in the autumn they're as fat as pigs; stuffed with milk powder and potatoes and goodness knows what, but it's just fat and it all comes off when you start working them."

"It's all so different from riding horses," I said, wondering who was right. "I mean Jean Morris, who teaches us at Marsden won't break a horse until it's three and a half and she's always saying you mustn't work them hard or ride them in stiff competitions until they're five."

"Well, of course, the work's quite different," said Mark. "We don't hack miles along the road or sit on their backs all day or ride them through heavy going and we're careful not to tire them out. But it's a tricky business; it's very easy to overdo things."

"And plenty of them do break down in training," said Jim, "from what you were telling me about last season."

"Yes, but if they're any good their racing life's a short one," said Mark, "and then they're off to stud."

Except that Katie put her snaffle on upside down, the tack was soon cleaned. Mark and Jim were so brisk and efficient, though they were talking, that Jon and I had to work about three times as fast as we do when we help at the riding school.

Friday was a much more cheerful day. It was soon known all over the stables that Alex had telephoned Mr Sinclair, who'd told him that Moonstruck was always lazy at home and never showed her real speed even in trials; she needed all the drama of the race-course itself to liven her up.

Mr Phelps lost his worried frown and hardly looked to see if we were dragging straw out on our feet as we left the loose-boxes. Cyril Redman, the travelling lad, kept making feeble jokes while Jenny and Felicity sang duets as they groomed the first lot. We were hanging about waiting for Angela, who had suddenly decided to come for a ride with us and Katie.

We'd been fussing about whether we were suitably dressed for riding at Eastcombe, debating whether riding coats were necessary or whether anoraks, which the apprentices wore, would do. But when we saw Angela we began to feel absurdly formal even in our anoraks! She wore leather chaps, three sweaters and a cowboy hat, and in spite of what the books say, a silver chain and all her rings. Angela's one of those people who always makes you feel as though you are the one who's incorrectly dressed and immediately I saw her I felt like jettisoning all my correct clothes and wished that we had not promised Mummy to wear our crash caps.

But though we admired her riding outfit we thought Angela quite mad on the downs. She rode everywhere at a flat-out gallop without bothering about the rest of us. Katie fell off three times. Princess Amelia puffed and Goldie was in such a state of excitement that he couldn't walk a step and flung his head about the whole time except when he was galloping. Angela seemed perfectly happy. She told us that she loved fast and excitable horses, that schooling made them well-behaved and dreary and that Katie must learn to stick on. I enjoyed myself for Princess Amelia remained calm and controllable but Jon found the electrified Chunky difficult to manage; in fact his arms were almost pulled out of their sockets. He said afterwards that Angela was a menace.

We didn't see Mark on Saturday morning; he and Cyril and Moonstruck had set off early for the racecourse. Alex went out with the first lot and then, leaving the second lot to Mr Phelps, changed into his tweed suit and left at speed in his sporty-looking Jaguar which seemed to be kept for race meetings. I asked Angela if her father ever took her racing. "It bores me," she said, "I hate it. Alex (she called him Alex, not Daddy or anything) spends hours and hours in the bar talking about which beastly horse is going to win. It's not so bad if he's got several horses running because then he has to keep going down to the paddock to give the jockeys their instructions and talk to the owners, but otherwise you're stuck in some dreary bar."

Then I asked, "Are you riding today?" and had quite a job to hide my relief when Angela said no, she was going to finish the dress she was making.

Out in the stables I found Bert and Katie and Jon already grooming. I told them that Angela had decided not to come. Jon and Katie looked distinctly relieved but Bert was rather annoyed and asked what was the use of keeping Goldie eating his head off for a girl who rode once a month.

Katie said she didn't want to go on the downs and that she knew a lovely ride along lanes and through a forest. "You can canter in the forest," she said, "the paths are covered with pine needles and Pincushion behaves himself so long as no one starts to race." We promised that we wouldn't race. I asked if she really knew the way or if we'd better take the map? And

38

Jon inquired suspiciously whether there was much road work?

"Not much," Katie answered. "A bit to Upton Greeley and then lanes to the forest. It's not a great lot of road work, is it, Bert?"

"No, and it won't do you no harm to take it steady either," Bert told us severely. "Galloping the poor animals off their feet yesterday by the look of them; it's always the same with Angela. No sense at all."

So we went for a calm and sedate ride, uneventful except that Pincushion almost lay down in the ford at Upton Greeley and then we took a wrong track in the forestry commission land and had to go back. Katie was very talkative and told us all about the accident which had caused Mark's limp.

"He fell out of a tree when he was ten," she said. "A really high tree and he broke both his legs, one in three places, and one of his wrists. He was in hospital for months. Six months, I think. That's what's made him small. Well, all his family are small, but he's the smallest."

"Poor Mark," I said. "Still, he's probably glad in some ways now he's decided to be a jockey."

"I wonder if he decided to become a jockey because he *was* small," said Jon.

"He liked riding too," Katie told us. "He rode a lot in gymkhanas and show jumping before he came here. Some boys, like Jimmy, haven't ridden at all. Dad gets furious at having to teach them—he's no good at it, that's why I have Mark to teach me."

Thinking of Mark we realised that it was after twelve and that he would have ridden his race.

"Oh, I do hope he's won," I said.

"He ought to have; Bert told me Moonstruck was favourite and the odds were so short it wasn't worth having a bet," Jon observed knowledgeably.

"Well, *I* heard Bert telling Mrs Hinde that if Dad doesn't have a winner soon we won't have a horse left in the stable," said Katie. "Angela would say 'Good riddance', but I expect Dad would mind," she added sadly.

We were late for lunch and Mrs Hinde had gone home. But Angela said that it didn't matter, she always went early on Saturdays and we would find our food on plates in the oven.

We found enormous helpings of fish pie and spinach and apple crumble. We'd finished, put everything in the dishwasher and were just making coffee when Geoff came in; there was a spitefully triumphant look on his broad, rosy-cheeked face.

"Heard the news?" he asked Angela. "Moonstruck was sixth—last but one. Brilliant piece of riding by Eastcombe's wonder boy."

Angela looked upset. "Truly, Geoff? You're not fooling?" she asked. "How did you hear?"

"My spies are everywhere," answered Geoff irritatingly. "The favourite finished sixth, you can't put it plainer than that."

Angela said, "Oh hell, Alex will be in a state." And then, trying to look unconcerned, she added, "Make yourself some coffee, Geoff."

"Well, perhaps it'll be an eye-opener for him," suggested Geoff. "Give your Dad a shake-up, make him see our Marky's not the blue-eyed boy he's always thought. I reckon old Mat Codling slipped Mark something not to ride Moonstruck out."

"Don't be stupid," Angela told him fiercely.

"I don't know about stupid, rather fly of Mark really. I suppose old Codling was sour at Sinclair changing stables and you see he trained the winner—Spanish Beach."

"You're just trying to stir up trouble. You know Mark wouldn't take a bribe," Angela told him.

Geoff shrugged his shoulders. "The stewards aren't so sure of his lily-whiteness or they wouldn't be holding an enquiry," he said, looking round at us to make sure his triumph was complete.

"They're not, are they?" Angela was almost beseeching him to tell her that it was all some silly joke and Geoff looked so pleased by what was evidently a disaster that it *was* difficult to believe him.

"Well, if you don't believe me, ask the others," he said. "They were all listening."

I wasn't enjoying watching Geoff playing cat and mouse with Angela, so I got off the kitchen table and said, "I'll go and find out." Jon followed me. As we crossed the yard he said, "This on top of what Katie was saying this morning doesn't look too good."

"No," I agreed, "I suppose that's why Angela's so upset. Supposing Mark is blamed, what happens?"

"Well, in most sports they suspend you or fine you," answered Jon.

The yard seemed empty of human life. Some of the horses were lying down, others munched contentedly at their hay, but we found Felicity and Jenny in the tack room, sitting on a bench both bent over a magazine called "Bride".

"Is it true about Mark and Moonstruck?" I asked. They didn't seem very perturbed. "She was sixth," said Felicity. "Well, that's the head-dress I should choose," she pointed out a photograph to Jenny.

"Is it true that the stewards are holding an enquiry?" I asked.

They both looked up. I could see that they were longing to say, "We're busy, buzz off and leave us in peace," but politeness stopped them. "Yes," said Jenny. "Well, there's bound to be really."

"If the favourite runs badly they have to look into it, don't they?" added Felicity.

"But if I had the Victorian style," said Jenny turning back to the magazine, "only with different sleeves—"

Jon and I left them and, went gloomily back to the kitchen. "Jenny and Felicity say it *is* true," I told Angela, but I could see that she knew, that Geoff had managed to convince her while we were away.

I drank the rest of my coffee and told Jon I was going to clean tack. I felt I had to get away from Geoff's look of triumph.

# CHAPTER FOUR

### KEEPING WATCH

IT wasn't until we were tack cleaning on Monday afternoon that we learned any more about the disastrous race. Jon, as usual, bluntly asked the question which tact would never have allowed me to hint at.

"What really happened in that race?" he asked. "We only heard Geoff's story."

"It was terrible," answered Mark, looking up from his saddle and blushing at the remembrance. "It was really horrible. You see, what Mr Sinclair said about her waking up when she got on the course didn't happen; she was just her usual sluggish self. We got away quite well but then I found the others were leaving me standing. I was pushing her along for all I was worth, I got my whip out at the end of the first furlong, I didn't know what else to do, she wouldn't go, or really it felt more as though she *couldn't* go. I couldn't get near the leaders."

"But what do you think was wrong?" I asked.

"I don't know." Mark shook his head miserably. "If I didn't know her form last season, I'd say she just didn't have it in her."

"I bet it was Geoff," said Jimmy, his voice bitter and his pale face tight and angry. "By the way he was going on, I bet he was mixed up in it somehow."

"But Moonstruck left here so early, hours before the race," Jon pointed out. "What could he have done?"

"Oh, there's no difficulty about drugs if you're in with the right people," answered Mark. "You can get hold of pep pills to make the horses go faster, every sort of tranquillizer and dope to slow them up. *And* you can get them fast acting or slow acting to suit your plans."

"And how do you give them?" I asked.

"In the feed or water, or you inject it," answered Mark, "or you can shove them down their throats on a balling stick or a wooden spoon, like electuary when

43

they have coughs. Geoff *could* have done it and he could have had friends on the course, but I'm not saying that he did, mind you."

"Course he did," muttered Jimmy.

"And what about the Stewards?" asked Jon. I gave him an angry look. No one wants to relate their humiliating moments to an audience and I could see that Mark minded. He was looking very hard at his stirrups and leathers as he put them back on his saddle. There was a silence and I think even Jon began to feel he had gone too far, but suddenly Mark spoke quite cheerfully.

"There were three of them," he said. "Old men in suits. They had angry eyes and you could see they felt certain I'd been mixed up in some dirty work, but they didn't know what to pin on me. No one could say I hadn't tried to ride Moonstruck out. They asked for an explanation. I said that I was just as puzzled as anyone else. Later they called me back and gave me a warning. I think Mr Grant got a warning too."

"I don't see why they should suspect you of *not* riding to win," I said. "Obviously you want to make a name as a jockey and Mr Grant wants to be a successful trainer, so what would be the point in losing?'

Mark thought for a moment and then said, "There could be money in it. Moonstruck being favourite there wasn't much to be won by backing her, but supposing you knew that she'd been got at, then you could put your money on the next best horse and get much better odds; it's done. And sometimes trainers or owners don't want a horse ridden right out at the beginning of the season. They plan to get better odds later on and make a kill when the horse is really

44

wound up and certain to win, but the public and the bookies don't know when that is; they're kept in the dark."

"What did Mr Sinclair say?" asked Jon.

"Couldn't make it out at all," answered Mark. "Couldn't account for it any more than anyone else. But old Mat Codling was there—he trained her, you know, till he and Mr Sinclair fell out—well, he came and looked at her afterwards in the stables and then I heard him talking to Mr Grant. 'Well, Alex, my boy,' he always talks like that, 'I know I can't teach you anything, but I should say you've got her a bit on the gross side; she's carrying a trifle more flesh than I like to see,' " imitated Mark in a plummy voice. "The course vet looked her over too," Mark added, "but he couldn't find anything wrong."

"Could it be that she was just too fat?" asked Jon.

Mark shook his head. "I don't think so. A good horse which wasn't fit would start well and then trail away; she was just uniformly slow. I never got her going. Oh well, it's not my pigeon any more," he said and began to clean his bridle briskly. "Mr Sinclair said to give me another chance, but the boss said 'certainly not!' He said if we'd learned anything from 'this fiasco' it was that she wasn't the horse for a boy, so that's that."

I felt very sorry for Mark. He was putting a good face on his troubles, but knowing that he was ambitious, and how much racing meant to him I could see that this must be a very real disaster to his plans and I wished I could think of something to do besides just being sympathetic.

On Monday evening Jon said he was going to be

45

constructive and borrowed my best notebook. There wasn't much in it, only some attempts at drawing horses and one feeble poem so I tore them out, and Jon sat on my bed making lists of people and their possible motives for doping Moonstruck. He wrote down Geoff's accusations against Mark as well as Jimmy's against Geoff, so it was Mark who came out with the blackest character as well as the most opportunity to do whatever had been done. I felt cross and said I didn't call that at all constructive, but simply a waste of my best notebook. But Jon, sucking his biro reflectively said that he could see why the stewards were suspicious, only they didn't know Mark as we did; they didn't realise how much he wanted to win.

Moonstruck's next race was at Canley Park. It was a three-day meeting. She was to run on the Wednesday and Costaway, one of Sandy's horses and Felicity's Snowsurf were running on the Thursday.

We heard that a very expensive jockey called Les Cooper had been engaged to ride Moonstruck. Everyone around the stableyard approved: they said he was "just the lad" and "if he can't boot her along no one can." Geoff was quite certain that Moonstruck would now return to her winning form and Felicity and Jenny kept on saying that "Poor old Mark was only a sixteen-year-old apprentice" and that "Mr Grant expected too much of him and it wasn't fair on the boy." I began to wonder if they were right and if we were making a great fuss about nothing. I liked Mark, but obviously that didn't mean I had to believe he was a good rider, only he seemed to have such confidence in himself and Alex evidently thought he was good. But perhaps Alex's judgment was faulty? Jon said I was on quite the wrong tack. He was certain there was a mystery and we must get up really early on Tuesday morning and be up on the downs to see if there were any suspicious characters hanging about when Les Cooper rode Moonstruck.

But if there were any suspicious characters about we missed them. Having no alarm clock we overslept and though we hurried like mad and even went without breakfast we reached the downs just as the first lot were leaving, their work done.

Furious with ourselves we went for a short ride but when we got back, Jon was even more furious because he had missed seeing Les Cooper's car which was apparently some fantastic foreign sports model. He heard about it from the boys, who were all wildly excited. I could see that even Mark was having fantasies about the car he would own when he was champion jockey.

I didn't care about the car, but when I tried to find out how Moonstruck had gone I found that everyone had been sworn, or rather threatened, to secrecy by Alex and we certainly didn't dare ask him. Cut off from the stable plans, Jon and I laid our own. We decided to keep watch on Tuesday night and at least make sure that Moonstruck left Eastcombe without being nobbled.

Jon's bedroom window gave quite a good view of the stableyard but we felt we would be too far away to identify shadowy figures creeping into loose-boxes nor would we be able to snatch hypodermic syringes and wooden spoons from their hands in time! So, after lunch, we went out and strolled round the yard pretending to talk to the horses but really spying out the land and searching for somewhere to spend the night.

Jon suggested that Moonstruck's box was the obvious place, but I thought that the presence of two strangers would keep her awake and might easily lose her the race next day. The tackroom and the feed house were both under the Phelps' flat at the top of the yard, so we felt they were a little dangerous, and anyway Moonstruck's box was the second of the ones on the left side as you entered the yard, so we wanted to be nearer. In the end we settled on an empty box on the right side opposite Moonstruck. There we were as far as possible from Mr Phelps and we would have a good view of anyone entering by the main gate though not such a good one of a person coming from the apprentices' dormitory on the other corner.

We made very thorough preparations for the adventure. We checked our torches and then went down to the village shop to buy provisions, mostly chocolate to eat and bitter lemon to drink. The nights were still very cold so we decided to wear three sweaters each under our anoraks, and then we began to think of weapons.

"The thing is," said Jon, "that we may be able to frighten the person off by making a noise, but supposing there's so much at stake that he's really *determined* to stick a hypodermic into her, how are we going to stop him? And then if he knows we've seen him he may decide that we're too dangerous to live, and then, of course, it mayn't be just one person, but a gang."

I'd been looking forward to our night on guard but now I began to feel afraid. Supposing this wasn't just a jealous plot to discredit Mark, but something much larger? Were we crazy to get mixed up in it, for how could *we* deal with a gang? I thought of what Mummy would say if Jon was bashed on the head. "You're the eldest, you should have stopped him," had always been a great cry in our family, though I must admit I'd heard it less often since Jon had grown taller than me. I asked myself if we were being idiots; but I couldn't see that we were. After all, if we solved the mystery of Moonstruck it could make all the difference to Mark's career and perhaps even to the future of Alex Grant's stable.

"Well, I suppose it'll have to be stout sticks," said Jon, who was following his own train of thought.

"Croquet mallets," I suggested and Jon agreed though he was also going to carry his knife and lumps of sugar for the petrol tank of the getaway car.

As dusk fell we placed the croquet mallets conveniently at the corner of the house and then we went to say goodnight to Katie who had begun to demand stories from us. When we'd escaped from her we watched television while Angela made her dress. She'd just finished it and was trying it on when Alex appeared to say that it was time for bed and that he was just going out to lock up. Angela, who was evidently in one of her defiant moods, said that the new dress was ghastly. She took it off, flung it in a corner and produced a crimson velvet curtain which was to provide material for her next effort. She soon had it draped round her, with me crawling on the floor putting in pins.

We had agreed, Jon and I, to keep watch from his room until the house slept, so I joined him there as soon as I thought Angela was safely in bed. I could

49

imagine the awkward enquiries if she met me in the passage, wearing an anorak. Jon was sitting at the window, having already started his share of the provisions.

"How are you going to survive the small hours when you're guzzling now and it's only eleven fifteen?" I demanded. Jon ignored my question and said, "The Phelps' light went out half an hour ago, Alex's has been out for twenty minutes, Angela's for five minutes and yours for fifty seconds." He'd written it all down in my best notebook. "How long are we going to give them?"

"Another half hour?" I suggested.

"Longer than that surely," said Jon. "After all no one's likely to attempt evil deeds before midnight."

"If I were an outsider I'd come between one and two," I agreed. "But if I worked here I'd know what time everyone went to bed. And if it's Geoff he might have a job to keep awake, so I think he'd come as soon as the other boys were asleep."

"Do you think someone's there watching the lights go out?" asked Jon. "If he is, mine went out just after Angela's."

I gave a shudder. I didn't like the idea of an unseen watcher. "He's bound to see us cross from the house to the yard with that large fat moon sailing about."

"We'll wait for a good moment. She keeps diving behind clouds and then it's quite dark; I've been watching her," said Jon.

We waited and waited. The night was full of a thick velvety quiet that wasn't silence. Besides the occasional stamp and scrape from the stable as horses got up or lay down, there was the wind in the trees and some twittering bird noises, a hunting owl on the down, a caterwauling cat in the village. Time passed very slowly and I began to feel that we were missing everything by being so far away. I imagined hunched figures creeping down the shadow by the left-hand loose-boxes. Moonstruck herself was invisible, lost in the gloom of her box.

Jon sighed, fidgetted and drew terribly bad pictures of racehorses and fast cars in my notebook by the light of the moon. Then he ate more of his chocolate.

Suddenly we both decided it was time to go. "They must be asleep by now," Jon whispered as we stuffed our pockets with provisions, took up our torches and crept out. There was only Angela's door to pass before we reached the stairs, but, as usual when you try to creep, the noise we made seemed tremendous. Jon's footfall sounded like thunder and when I stepped on a loose board it gave a sort of creaky squawk. We both waited frozen in horror for Rom to leap off Kate's bed and rush out barking loudly. Nothing happened. The house slept on. We could hear clocks ticking but that was all. The front door opened easily; we left the latch up for our return at five-thirty. The gravel scrunched noisily as we crept along the house, hoping that the half-veiled moon wouldn't reveal us. We collected the croquet mallets and hurried across the open space to the stable gates. They were chained and padlocked. Alex Grant's nightly locking up, I thought, but they were perfectly easy to climb at the lowest point where the two gates met.

Half-way over Jon dropped his croquet mallet with a clatter that brought several horse heads to the loose-box doors. Someone, I think it was Handout, gave a

51

"*We collected the croquet mallets and hurried
to the stable.*"

little whinny and, of course, the moon chose that moment to race out from behind a cloud and illuminate us. I felt terribly exposed standing there waiting for one of Mr Phelps' windows to be thrown up and an angry voice to demand what we were up to. Nothing happened. I climbed over and followed Jon to the loose-box. We inspected it by torchlight. There was a manger—nothing else. The floor was swept clean. We bolted the door and then stood looking out across the yard. The quality of the light changed continually as the wind blew broken clouds across the sailing moon The shadows in the yard quivered, lengthened, shortened and were never still. It was an exciting night and you could see the horses thought so too. Innocent-looking two-year-old heads appeared at intervals, and gazed out with passionate interest, sometimes snorting softly to themselves.

It was midnight. Presently my legs started to ache and still no figure crept towards the ghostly patch of grey that was Moonstruck standing in her box. "Supposing we take it in turns to watch?" I suggested to Jon. "The other one could sit on the manger and go to sleep." He agreed. "All right, half an hour each. You can have first sleep if you like."

We wound our watches and then I sat in the manger, which was hard and cold but warmed up gradually, and imagined myself riding in a race. It's mean that the Newmarket Town Plate is the only race for girls. I imagined us catching the doper red-handed and Alex being so delighted that he persuaded one of his rich owners to mount me for the race. I wondered if the horses had to be any special age or I a special weight. Then I must have dozed off, for the next thing

I knew was Jon shaking me and saying that it was one o'clock and would I take over.

I was icy cold. I wished we'd brought coffee in a thermos and not bitter lemon, but I felt better when I'd eaten the rest of my chocolate. I stood at the door forcing my eyes to stay open to watch for the horse doper, then suddenly I found that I didn't believe in him any more. It was quite clear that we were behaving ridiculously; of course no one was going to creep in. Obviously Alex wasn't as good a trainer as Mat Codling, obviously Mark was a less experienced rider than the previous jockey. A deep depression fell upon me. I wondered what would happen if Eastcombe stables had no more winners? If all the owners took their horses away? Supposing Alex went bankrupt, what would happen to Angela and Katie? Well, Angela was old enough to get a job, but Katie? I was glad our parents weren't divorced. It was difficult to imagine life other than it was, but I was sure I wouldn't want to be Angela. I must write to Mummy and Daddy, I thought. I'll write tomorrow, no it's really today. I may have some exciting news. I'd begun to believe in the horse doper again. I watched and my brain grew numb, groaning for sleep and my heavy eyes had to be bullied to search the shadows effectively. Half-past one passed. Jon was asleep. I gave him extra time as he had me. I'd wake him at a quarter to two, I decided. And then the noise began.

Bang, bang, bang. Jon woke at once. "What on earth?" he demanded joining me at the door.

"Shush! I don't know, it's only just started!" We listened as the banging went on. My heart banged as well and almost as loudly.

The noise was coming from the other side of the yard, not from Moonstruck's box but one more in the middle; one of Sandy's horses or Geoff's?

We grabbed our croquet mallets, ran across the yard and shone our torches into a box. A startled horse backed nervously away. The banging began again in the next box. We looked in. A large brown horse was lying on his side kicking the wall of the box with his feet. He was obviously upset, he threshed about wildly and was already sweating with fright.

"Has he broken his leg or something?" asked Jon as we went in.

"Could it be colic?" I suggested remembering Pony Club lectures, but I'd never seen a horse with it.

The horse continued to thresh wildly, he seemed to be trying to get on his feet. We tried to help, pushing at his back, but he seemed to be too near the wall and when we tried to move his legs his flailing hoofs were too near our heads for comfort and we retreated. "We need a rope," said Jon, "I'll look in the tack room."

"And a head collar," I called after him.

The horse went into another violent struggle. I could see he was going to hurt himself so I went to his head and tried to calm him down. It worked for a bit, he lay still, trembling and sweating, but then he began to struggle and bang with renewed violence.

Jon came running back to say that the tack room was locked but Mr Phelps' light had gone on. I knew that we ought to run for it, that awkward questions would be asked, but the struggling horse and the noise confused me. I went on saying, "Whoa boy, it's all right, Mr Phelps is coming," until Mr Phelps, an old raincoat over striped pyjamas, did come and a second later Alex, a sheepskin coat over orange pyjamas, hurried in breathlessly.

"It's The Giant, cast," said Mr Phelps pushing Jon towards the door, and the two men advanced on the struggling horse and grabbing his tail high up where the bone is they tugged and tugged. Gradually inch by inch they pulled him round away from the wall until The Giant, finding his legs freed, scrambled up. He stood there, his rug askew, trembling. I patted him while Mr Phelps unbuckled the rug and roller and then he and Alex inspected one side each for damage. There were no obvious wounds.

"Thank God *he's* not running tomorrow," said Alex.

"He's such a great gawky chap. They're the ones that get cast as a rule," said Mr. Phelps re-rugging The Giant. "You great silly."

With all the patting and talking and general attention The Giant began to recover from his horrible experience—he reached out for a mouthful of hay.

Alex inspected us critically. "First on the scene *and* fully dressed?" he said. Jon and I looked at each other and I had a horrible feeling that my face was just as red and guilty-looking as his. We both mumbled vaguely about being awake, but then, as we left the box, there were our croquet mallets lying in the yard.

"A midnight croquet match?" suggested Alex sarcastically. He went quietly to Moonstruck's box, looked in and then rejoined us.

Mr Phelps said, "Good night all," and then looked at his watch and corrected himself, "No, good morning."

We climbed the gate and Alex, following us over,

asked, "Are you two becoming involved in stable politics? Because if so, I'd rather you didn't."

I was still trying to think of an answer to this when he spoke again. "Did any of the lads ask you to do this? Did Mark or any of the others ask you to give anything to the horses? I mean carrots or sugar, anything at all?"

"*No*, of course not." I answered indignantly. "Mark didn't even know we were staying up."

"We were watching for a horse doper," explained Jon. "We decided something odd was going on, that's why we stayed up."

"And you proposed to knock him out with croquet mallets?" asked Alex mockingly.

"They were for self-defence," answered Jon, who seemed to be keeping his head. Filled with a mixture of humiliation and rage I felt more like bursting into tears.

"Well, keep out of it," said Alex. "If there *is* anything going on it won't make a glamorous adventure; it'll just be a nasty, sordid, money-making little racket. I've been in racing long enough to know."

At the top of the stairs Alex whispered, "Sleep well," and Jon and I crept despondently back to our rooms.

# CHAPTER FIVE

### A HORRIBLE IDEA

WE slept late next morning. In fact we were awakened by Katie who came bouncing into our rooms to tell us that it was ten o'clock and to deliver the long-awaited postcards from Russia. Mine was of the Kremlin, Jon's of the Red Square. Mummy had written them. "Having a wonderful time. Daddy's working hard and I'm seeing the sights with another wife. Lots of parties so I'm wearing the new clothes. Hope you are enjoying yourselves and being sensible. Love to Alex, Angela and Katie. And lots to you, Mummy." Jon's had a bit about there being almost no private cars in Moscow and how easy it was to cross the roads. Well, we weren't being sensible and I wasn't going to give any love to Alex, I thought bitterly as I recalled the incidents of the night before. But it was nice to be reminded that we were only temporary visitors at Eastcombe—presently we would go home leaving the scene of our errors and misjudgments.

Katie, who was running between our rooms, took Jon's postcard to him and brought back mine, then she sat down on my bed and said, "Is it true?"

"What?" I asked.

"Dad said I was to let you sleep on as you'd spent the whole night chasing gangs of horse-dopers round the stable yard and hitting them with croquet mallets."

"No," I said firmly, "it's not. All that happened was that The Giant got cast."

"Oh, was that all. I thought Dad was telling tall stories. Well, you can get up now then. Mark's gone racing with Moonstruck so I've no one to give me a lesson and Jimmy wants one too."

"A lesson?" I asked in horror.

"Yes, why not?" she asked, "this afternoon. You and Jon ride quite well, everyone says so, so you must be able to instruct us. You can do it separately or both together—we don't mind."

I agreed to dress, so she went off to bully Jon. When we reached the kitchen Mrs Hinde wasn't at all pleased to see us. She said that we were catching Angela's bad habits.

After breakfast we went out to see our horses. I felt rather guilty the way we left them to Bert. At least Jon shared Chunky, but Princess Amelia had been borrowed entirely for my benefit and I felt that I ought to look after her. But since they had obviously been fed and watered and they stood in beautifully clean stables there was nothing to do but agree to Katie's demand for a game of croquet. It was lunch time when Angela and Bert returned from shopping in Longbridge and in the middle of lunch Angela asked, "Is it true what Alex said about—"

"No," I interrupted quickly, but that idiot Jon blundered in with, "Is what true?"

"Alex says you spent the night driving off doping gangs with croquet mallets," explained Angela.

Jon went scarlet in the face but I was getting hardened to it. "No, we were just keeping an eye open and then The Giant got cast," I told her.

"Well, Alex's parting words were 'For God's sake keep the Bradleys out of mischief,'" said Angela. "But I don't know what he expects *me* to do. Anyway, I think people should decide things for themselves. Not perhaps at Katie's age, but from about twelve onwards."

Jon and I sat awkward and speechless but luckily Katie filled the gap. "They're giving me and Jimmy a lesson this afternoon," she said.

"Do you think they really want to?" asked Angela doubtfully.

"Of *course* they do," answered Katie. "It's all fixed. "I do hope Pincushion's in a good mood, I want to jump one foot nine."

When Pincushion was ready there was still no sign of Jim so the three of us wandered across the yard to see if he really wanted a lesson as Katie swore he did. During the racing season the stable staff who weren't actually at the races were generally free after lunch until evening stables at four-thirty. The men who were married and had cottages nearby stayed at home gardening or something and, according to Mark, Mr Phelps always had a sleep. Jenny and Felicity sat in the tack room listening to the radio and knitting while the boys were supposed to amuse themselves in the room next to their dormitory where they had table tennis and television; but Mark said that they mostly lay on their beds and smoked which was dull and he preferred to ride. This afternoon they certainly weren't lying on their beds. Sandy was holding Jimmy on the ground while Brian hosed him and Geoff stood by laughing and egging them on. Jimmy, absolutely awash with water, was screaming with what sounded more like rage and frustration than fright.

Since there were three of them and they had the hose I didn't see much hope of making a rescue. Nor did Jon seem disposed to start a fight so I decided to try persuasion. "Please let him come now," I asked. "we're all waiting to ride."

Brian sprayed a little water over us and another torrent over Jimmy, then said to Sandy, "Let him go and have his bit of riding practice. If anyone needs it he does."

Sandy, who was almost as wet as his victim, let go, but Jim, leaping up with a hoarse cry of rage, threw himself upon Brian and started the fight again.

"Give him another wetting, he hasn't cooled down yet," shouted Geoff and with that water shot all over the yard, frightening several of the horses as Jim and Brian struggled. Jon ran to the tap and turned it off. Then he and I levered Jim off Brian and, despite jeers from Geoff and Sandy, we persuaded him to go and change.

We waited because it was obvious that if we didn't it would all start up again when Jim reappeared. We sat on feed tins talking to Brian and Sandy; Geoff was too superior to take much notice of us. I liked Brian best; he had long straight hair and a monkey face.

I don't think Jim enjoyed his ride much; he was too miserable, but Katie jumped one foot nine inches several times and was very pleased with herself. Jon and I took it in turns to instruct and ride. We gave Jim a jump or two on Princess Amelia, which was a great success and did cheer him up slightly.

Mark and Moonstruck were home in time for evening stables so we joined the general rush to hear what had happened. Cyril Redman and Mark both explained at once that Moonstruck had been last, despite frantic efforts on Les Cooper's part. Afterwards the stewards had ordered a dope test, which the racecourse vet had carried out, but it would be several days before the result was known. Everyone felt very dismal on hearing this as we gathered that Alex could lose his licence to train if the test was positive.

Mark was as gloomy as everyone else and showed no signs of triumph that a jockey of Les Cooper's experience had equalled his devastating failure with Moonstruck.

"I think Mr Grant suspects I'm responsible," he said bitterly when everyone had gone to do his own horses and only Jon and I were left at the door of Moonstruck's box.

"Responsible?" I repeated in surprise.

"Yes, for doping her—if she was doped."

"Oh, I don't believe that," said Jon.

"He asked me a lot of questions after the race," Mark went on, ignoring our doubt. "They were all put in the nicest possible way, you know, sort of fatherly. Did I know anything at all about what was going on? If I *had* got mixed up in anything I was to be sure to tell him. Was I in any trouble over money? I was only young so much could be forgiven me that in an older person . . . Oh, I don't know, it all pointed the same way; if Moonstruck *was* doped he thinks I'm up to the neck in it."

I didn't know what to say; I felt powerless under the weight of Mark's bitterness and depression.

Jon said, "But it's obvious that you must be the

chief suspect because you've got the most opportunity. If anyone else wanted to get at Moonstruck's food and water he'd have to distract your attention or get you out of the way first. You're a key character in the whole mystery."

"Yes, I see that," agreed Mark, "but Mr Grant didn't put it like that. It was all this 'Confide in me, my boy' stuff—well, it was nearly as bad as that—which got me down. He even asked me if I'd put you up to charging round the yard with croquet mallets at one o'clock this morning."

I felt embarrassed and Jon looked it. "We were only keeping an eye on things," I said, "and we told him that it was nothing to do with you or anyone else."

"He seems to think I'm using you to stir up a flap about outsiders while I do the dirty work myself."

"Oh Mark, he can't think that," I said. "We told him it was all our own idea and, besides, he likes you."

"He used to," answered Mark slinging on Moonstruck's rug. "Now he thinks I've gone wrong. Anyway my ride on High Jester's off," he added, his face hidden as he buckled the roller, but his voice telling us what a grievous disappointment this was.

Mark gathered up his grooming tools without looking at us. We followed him to High Jester's box. I was waiting for him to volunteer some more information but Jon burst in with a question, "Where and when were you going to ride High Jester?" he asked.

"Well, it wasn't exactly settled," Mark answered as he whipped off High Jester's rug, "but you see I broke him and schooled him, and I've done him since he came as a yearling. He goes well for me and Mr Grant always said said unless the owner had any strong feelings about it he thought I should ride him in his first race. Now he says that with all this hanging over us he doesn't feel he can talk the owner into putting me up." Mark patted High Jester's neck. "It isn't *just* that I want the ride on him. He's a clever colt, but nervous and I know he'd go better for someone he's used to first time out." Mark's voice broke again but he continued to body brush with feverish vigour.

"It's all so silly," I said angrily. "Alex *must* know you wouldn't dope Moonstruck."

"Once you get a bad name in racing it sticks, that's the real trouble," Mark told us sadly. "Doesn't matter whether you deserved it or not; it sticks. The trainers all go round saying there's no smoke without fire and that's the end of you. I'm beginning to feel like packing the whole thing in. If Mr Grant agrees I could go home and start working to get into a technical college or something—that would please my father, he's always been against racing."

Alex came home earlier than usual that evening and he, too, wore a gloomy face. He came up to say goodnight to Katie while I was reading one of those dreary stories about a princess who can't decide whom to marry. He didn't say anything then, but later, when we had gone down to watch television, he pounced on us and asked, "I imagine you've heard the stewards ordered a dope test?"

"Of course they have," answered Angela. "It's the only subject of conversation in this place."

"You two were expecting something to happen last night," Alex went on, "I'd very much like to know who put that idea into your heads."

Jon and I looked at each other. "We thought of it ourselves, didn't we?" I asked Jon.

Alex made a sceptical face. "Two weeks ago you didn't know that horses were doped."

"I think it was Jimmy," I said, remembering the discussion in the saddle room. "He was convinced that Geoff was behind it all, that he was giving Moonstruck buckets of water or tranquillizers to slow her up so that Mark gets a bad name. But, now that the same thing has happened with Les Cooper riding . . . well, it alters everything."

"You mean you were waiting to knock a member of my staff on the head with a croquet mallet?" asked Alex in a surprised voice.

"No, the mallets were for self-defence and we had open minds about whether it was an insider or outsider we were watching for," answered Jon. "And if it wasn't spite then the motive must have been money. Mark says if you know the favourite's been got at you can make money backing the second best horse, well that applies to anyone inside or outside a stable."

Alex pounced on Jon's words. "Mark told you that, did he?"

"Only because we were being thick-headed and couldn't understand why he should be suspected of not riding Moonstruck to win," I explained hastily.

"Well, if you know anything or learn anything or if you hear of any of the boys having more spending money than usual I want you to tell me at once. Don't stick nobly to schoolboy codes of not sneaking because this isn't a schoolboy situation."

"They all seem permanently broke," said Jon.

"And I'm sure it wasn't Mark," I began, then I

tried to stop my voice sounding so indignant and began again. "I'm sure Mark wants to win races, he doesn't care about money, he wants to be a first-class jockey."

"And what would he do with money?" Jon backed me up. "He's not old enough to buy a car."

"He could have got into trouble of some sort, it's easy enough in the racing world. If a shady character wants a boy in his grasp he can soon engineer it, I promise you," said Alex. "That's one of the reasons I want you two to keep right out of it all, so *please* no more nocturnal adventures."

"Well, there's no point now," Jon answered. "I mean there can't be any advantages left in doping a non-favourite. And anyway, when is Moonstruck's next race?"

"That," said Alex in a very non-committal voice, "remains to be seen."

As we went up to bed Jon said, "Come to my room a minute, I want to talk and mine's more private than yours." So I followed him along the passage and shut the door. "What is it?" I asked. "Hurry up because I'm sleepy and squint-eyed with television."

"I've got a new idea," said Jon looking serious. "Rather a horrible one really. He produced my best notebook and seeing that I wasn't going to get anything out of him quickly I collapsed on his bed, but his first words made me sit up again.

"Has it occurred to you that it would be just as easy for him to have done it as for Mark?"

"Him?" I asked.

"Alex," whispered Jon melodramatically.

"Just as easy, well, almost as easy," I agreed, "but

there's no point, why on earth should he? He's only wrecking his name as a trainer by losing races."

"But if he was practically bankrupt, if he has no money left for hay bills or staff or anything else he might let a horse lose in order to win a huge sum of money. If he put his last hundred pounds on Spanish Beach he'd have won a thousand."

"He doesn't seem any richer," I said feebly as I tried to think up a good argument against Jon's theory; I didn't want Alex to be a crook.

"He won't, not for months, he's far too clever to make an obvious mistake like that," observed Jon.

"I'm too sleepy to think," I said, "but I'm sure that he's not the doper." After all he is a life-long friend of Daddy's, I told myself.

"But don't you see that he's trying to pin it on Mark?" Jon demanded indignantly. "And why do you suppose he objects to us poking our noses in and wandering about the place?"

"Well, he is responsible for us and he says that he doesn't want us mixed up with the sordid underworld."

Jon snorted disbelievingly. "Have you noticed the pile of bills on the hall table?" he asked.

"How do you know they're bills, they may be receipts," I pointed out. "Anyway, he's bound to have bills, but it doesn't mean that he's broke."

"You've got to admit that Angela's worried and there's a feeling in the air that things are going wrong," said Jon.

"Yes, I do, but having no mother and being responsible for Katie and the shopping is enough to worry anyone," I answered. "I would hate to be in charge of everything at home. I wouldn't know how much of anything to buy."

"Yes, it would be a hideous muddle," agreed Jon complacently.

I lay awake for hours that night thinking about it all. I was sure that Mark wasn't the villain, my bones told me that he was honest and my head agreed; he wanted to ride winners and make a name for himself far more than he wanted money. Besides, I felt that if he was in the grasp of some gang he would be far more worried and nervous than he appeared. As for Alex, I didn't like him as much as I liked Mark nor did I know him so well. I could see that he might easily lose thousands on a horse and that then it would be tempting to fix a race so that he could win thousands back again, but he was Daddy's friend and the father of Katie and Angela. It would be a terrible disaster for them. Supposing Moonstruck *was* doped and he was convicted and went to prison? It was a really horrible situation. I began to wish that we'd never come to Eastcombe. I thought how lovely it would be if the parents came home early and whisked us away. Then I decided that I would try to dissuade Jon from collecting evidence against Alex. It would be much better to keep out of it unless, of course, he tried to make Mark the scapegoat—then we would have to act.

# CHAPTER SIX

### JIMMY DISAPPEARS

WHEN you've been having critical thoughts about people they have a horrible habit of staying with you afterwards and getting in the way. Both Jon and I felt very uncomfortable meeting Alex after our night of suspicion and as he didn't seem to be going racing as early as usual—both Snowsurf and Castaway were running in the late afternoon—we decided to take ourselves off for a long ride.

Princess Amelia was beginning to go marvellously. She was much fitter and the doormat coat was coming out in handfuls so instead of puffing and sweating and feeling tired she was always suggesting canters and gallops. Her suggestions were very polite ones; there was no fighting or prancing about sideways or refusing to walk, which was how Goldie made his desires known.

As we rode I stopped wishing for our parents' return. I don't mean that I didn't want them to come back, but it was just that I began to realise how much I was going to miss the downs. They were so large and windswept and beautiful in their bleak way. And they offered a sort of freedom that didn't exist in Marsden, where you always saw the end of a canter before you started. Here you stopped because you wanted to not because you had to; I can't explain it better than that.

"I wish we could move to the country," I said to Jon.

"And have a racing stable?" he asked.

"No, I'd be quite content with Princess Amelia," I answered. "Would you have Chunky?"

"Like a shot if he was given to me, but if I was going to buy a horse I'd choose something taller and faster. A cross between High Jester and Chunky."

In the afternoon the usual quiet descended on the stables. Mark on Goldie and Katie on Pincushion went off on some special, private trip which Katie had planned. They were to buy sweets at the village shop and visit one of her friends; all rather dreary roadwork, but Mark said that Goldie needed slow exercise and that he didn't mind. Jon and I cleaned our tack, rather sketchily as there were no experts looking, and then we lay in the sun and read.

It wasn't until evening stables that there was any sign of anything being wrong. Mark and Katie were late back, as Katie's friend's mother had insisted on giving them tea. This put Mark in a great flap, he said that they were very short-handed in the stables and all doing spares, so Jon and I offered to do Goldie. When we'd done him and helped Katie with Pincushion we went round the yard and found them all in a state over Jimmy. He had left after lunch saying that he was just going to the village and no one had seen him since.

"And you and I know why," said Jenny to us. "The poor little devil had had enough of these great louts. Tease, tease, tease, morning, noon and night." She turned on Geoff, "You ought to be ashamed of yourself, but I don't suppose you are, too blooming insensitive to feel *anything*."

"But we were only mucking around with the hose,"

protested a worried-looking Brian. "I don't see why he has to run away over a bit of fun like that."

"Fun," snorted Jenny angrily and thumped down a water bucket.

"Look, Jen, these sensitive little flowers like Jimmy don't have no place in racing stables. If he wants handling as though he was precious china he should work in an office," Geoff told her.

"'Course he should," agreed Brian.

"He'd be all right if you left him alone. And goodness only knows what you've driven him to now," Jenny shouted at Geoff. "If anything's happened to him, you'll be to blame."

Geoff began to shout insults back. Hearing them, Bert hurried out of the feed room uttering calming if disjointed sentences. "He'll be back. Nothing to worry about. Ten to one he hitched into Longbridge and missed the bus home. I reckon he's footing it now and in a rare old state knowing our Jimmy."

"He is only half an hour late," I said.

"Yes, it's a bit soon to get worked up about it," agreed Jon.

Mark said, "Lads aren't late for evening stables."

"No, well you can't be," explained Brian. "I mean you can't muck about with racehorses' feeding times and you can't expect other people to do your horses."

"And you risk being half murdered by old Phelps," added Geoff.

"Yes, and you'd have to be half dead in Longbridge hospital before *he'd* think you had an adequate excuse," agreed Mark.

We helped, filling water buckets, carrying hay in

71

split sacks, terrified lest we spilled one wisp on Mr Phelps' perfectly swept yard. No one would let us groom or rug up; they seemed to think us incapable, but when feed time came and there was still no sign of Jim we were allowed to tip the carefully measured feeds into Pressed Steel's and Rebel Rose's mangers.

Mr Phelps was looking worried and muttering about accidents and telephoning the police. He discussed the matter with Jenny and Bert and finally agreed with Jenny that probably Jim had run away. "Best wait till the Guv'nor gets back," he decided. "But if any of you sees or hears anything of him I want to know at once."

The stable work had finished late and Mrs Phelps was leaning out of a window calling that tea was spoiling, so we didn't have a chance to ask Mark any private questions. We hurried to the house to tell Angela and Katie what had happened. Angela didn't seem very interested. "Sensible boy," she said, "I'd run away if I was expected to spend my life looking after beastly racehorses."

Katie said hopefully that perhaps he had had an accident and was in hospital, and if so would we take her to see him?

Later that evening, when we were watching television, we heard the horsebox drive into the yard and neither Jon nor I could resist the temptation to rush out and ask how the horses had gone.

Sandy's pale, rather expressionless face was lit up with excitement as he told the group gathered round the loose-box door how Castaway had won, beating the favourite by a length. Felicity was pleased with

Snowsurf who'd run well and come third in good company. After we'd heard their stories we asked for news of Jim, but there was none. We were still in chattering groups when Alex drove up, and as Mr Phelps advanced on him we returned to the house and television.

Presently Alex came in. He looked more cheerful than usual so I supposed that Castaway's win had done the stable and his finances some good.

"Well, have the resident detectives any line on Jimmy King's disappearance?" he asked.

I was rather insulted by the patronising tone of voice but Jon was so pleased to be consulted that he didn't seem to notice.

"The general idea is that he's run away. He certainly was very upset yesterday, but they only soaked him. It wasn't as though they really *hurt* him. I thought he was making a bit of a fuss," said Jon.

"Jenny says they never stop teasing him," I pointed out.

"Yes, I'm afraid he's a born victim," said Alex. "Wherever he goes it'll be the same."

"But I'm not so sure that he has run away," Jon went on, "because I think he would have said something to Mark."

"And Mark says he won't have gone home because he's unhappy there and hates his stepfather," said Alex. "Well, we'll soon find out," and he headed for his office.

Later he put his head round the door and said, "Jim hasn't turned up at home yet and the police haven't picked up any bodies so we must just wait and

73

hope that morning brings an explanation. Isn't it time you people were in bed?"

"Do you think that this could be mixed up with Moonstruck in any way?" asked Jon thoughtfully.

"*No*," exploded Alex so loudly and firmly that I jumped. "Definitely not and I don't want any more night sessions with croquet mallets."

"I've been thinking over what you said last night," Jon told him calmly. "About boys getting into trouble. It would be much more likely to happen to Jim than to Mark. I mean he'd be easy to manipulate and once he was in trouble he wouldn't know how to get out of it."

Alex sighed, came in and sat down. "True," he said. "But then I don't believe in this all-powerful dope gang that you and Vivien have dreamed up. I think it's possible that Jim's got into debt; he seems to owe Geoff some money, but he hasn't been here long enough to get very deep into anything and I can't believe that any self-respecting gang would employ him, because I can't imagine a weaker link. Anyway, he'll either turn up at home or be picked up by the police. He hasn't much money on him, so he'll have to sleep rough and he looks such a child I can't see anyone giving him even temporary work."

I'd stopped thinking about Jimmy; a much more selfish idea had occurred to me and when we were outside the sitting-room door on our way to bed, I told Jon. "If Jimmy isn't back tomorrow morning they'll have a terrific lot of spares. Do you think he'd let us ride exercise?"

Jon looked at me in amazement and then he said, "*Yes*. Why not? We may as well *ask*."

"What, now?" I said, rather horrified.

"Yes, go on. You ask."

"No, you ask for a change," I told him. "You always make me do the difficult asking."

But Jon had already opened the sitting-room door and was pushing me in. Alex and Angela were watching the news. "What is it? Dopers under the bed?" he suggested.

"No, we were just wondering whether you might need some extra riders tomorrow," I mumbled nervously. "If Jimmy's not back, that is."

"She means for exercising," added Jon from behind the door. "We're not much good, but Jimmy only rides the quiet ones."

"Is this a genuine offer to exercise or merely a ruse for collecting inside information and detecting dopers?" asked Alex.

"Genuine," answered Jon and I together.

"You must be mad," observed Angela. "It's terribly dull."

"We've never ridden racehorses," I pointed out, "and I don't suppose we'll ever get the chance again."

"All right," said Alex. "Second lot," and he turned back to the television.

Jon and I rushed upstairs to my room controlling our desire to leap and shout because of Katie. Jon flung himself on my bed. "We're going to ride racehorses," he announced in a voice of triumph, mercifully muffled by eiderdown. "We're going to ride *racehorses*!"

We were up early next morning and learned with mixed feelings that Jimmy hadn't returned. No one seemed to need our help, even our ponies were munching large feeds, so there was nothing to do but cook our breakfasts. I was beginning to feel much less enthusiastic about riding racehorses. I could see Jon or myself committing some unforgivable error, like falling off and letting go of the reins.

Katie soon appeared in pyjamas demanding an omelette and news of Jimmy. When she found there was no news she began to invent ghastly accidents which might have happened to him and which she enjoyed with a heartless relish which rather shocked Jon and me.

Time passed very slowly. We made our beds and cleaned our boots, which wasn't really necessary as none of the stable staff bothered much about appearances when they were exercising, though they always looked very smart when they took their horses to race meetings. We groomed our ponies and rescued Katie when Pincushion trod on her toe; he was standing on it, eating hay and ignoring her cries of rage and pain. We restored our strength with coffee and biscuits and then, seeing the first lot come back, we went round to the stable yard.

We watched the first lot being strapped vigorously. It was mostly body-brushing and wisping for they were already spotlessly clean. When they had been given hay, the second lot were brushed over. We offered to help but our offers were swept aside as everyone flew around with an air of super efficiency. So we stood, feeling useless and becoming more and more apprehensive.

Abruptly the grooming stopped and quarter sheets, saddles and bridles went on. The second lot were ready. Mr Phelps came across to us. "Jon, you're having one of Jimmy's horses, Rosie, the black filly," he said. "And Vivien, you're having Mount Olive, one of Fred's, so if you go across he'll put you up."

Mount Olive looked huge. He was a red-golden chestnut with a really beautiful thoroughbred head, a silken mane and tail and a coat so fine it hardly seemed a coat.

Fred said, "He's a lovely ride. You'll be all right on him." He pulled down the stirrups, which hardly looked long enough for a dwarf and prepared to leg me up.

"How tall is he?" I asked, gazing up at the distant saddle.

"Sixteen-two, nothing really, and he rides like a pony," said Fred, seizing my leg and propelling me into the air. To my surprise and relief I found myself sitting in the saddle. I began to fiddle with the leathers.

"Don't try and ride short if you're not used to it," advised Fred, so I let them down to my usual jumping length. Then I was sent to walk round the grass plot in the centre of the yard until the rest of the string was ready. Jenny on Darkest Dawn, Mark on High Jester and Geoff on The Giant, were already circling the grass plot; I joined on a couple of lengths behind Geoff. Brian fell in behind me, Sandy was being legged up on to Pressed Steel. Then came Felicity on Secret Battle, Jon on Rebel Rosie, and last of all, Fred on Old Flame. We all walked round while Mr Phelps inspected us from a distance. You could see his eyes checking that bridles fitted, girths were tight enough and as Alex appeared at the gate he said, "All ready, sir."

"Thank you, Ken. Off you go then, Jenny," said

77

Alex. He, too, inspected us as we filed by. It may have been only the horses he was inspecting but I felt quite glad that I had cleaned my boots. We walked slowly down the drive. Mount Olive's neck was immensely long, his ears seemed miles away and his stride was so long it was almost like slow motion. Mark looked round and smiled, so I supposed I looked all right and then Geoff turned in his saddle.

"Still there, Viv? Give us a shout if he puts you down."

"He won't," called Jenny from the front. "Mount Olive's a perfect gentleman unlike some of the boys here."

Geoff shouted back an insult and then turned to me again. "Fred's other horse, Saturday Morning, is a proper pig. Puts you down every chance he gets and he's mean in the stable too. If he gets you in a corner he lets you have it."

"Yeah, Fred ought to have danger money doing Saturday Morning," agreed Brian from behind.

I looked round for Jon. He seemed quite at home, not as perched up as the other riders but quite efficient-looking.

We didn't talk much on the road. I was occupied in keeping my distance, Mount Olive was inclined to overhaul The Giant, and the riders of the two-year-olds had to concentrate on their wavering mounts. Geoff talked to The Giant a lot and I could hear Brian singing pop songs softly to Fortune's Favour, a very ugly, lop-eared two-year-old.

When we reached the downs the Land-Rover appeared from behind us and Alex, Mr Phelps and

Cyril joined us on a mowed and rolled stretch of turf at the beginning of the gallops. Jenny led us round in a large circle. I had grown used to Mount Olive's walk, but when the word to trot came down the line I was amazed by the length and springiness of his stride. There was a slight outburst of excitement ahead of me. The Giant gave a buck, High Jester plunged forward, but Mount Olive simply watched with interest. The two-year-olds' high spirits soon left them; they began to flounder with exhaustion and the order came to walk. We changed the rein and presently trotted again but not for long; then Alex and Mr Phelps consulted and we walked round. The sun was coming out and the air smelled delicious, as air beside a waterfall smells, sparkling and new. High in the faintly blue sky larks were singing and in the distance I could hear the bleat of lambs and the baa of sheep. Mount Olive was going well and I was enjoying myself. I looked back for Jon and seeing me turn, he waved, so I knew he was all right.

Alex was calling out people in threes and giving them their instructions. Mr Phelps was tightening girths so I could see that the real business of the morning was about to begin. I began to feel apprehensive again. Supposing I got Mount Olive galloping, was I ever going to be able to stop again?

Jon was going with Jenny and Fred Wells. I was called in with Mark and Geoff. "Now you three are going six furlongs and as both the two-year-olds have races coming up I want you to send them along. Vivien, you're on an old horse so you're the pace setter. I want you to ride at a canter for the first three furlongs, a half-speed gallop for the next two and then

79

gradually slow up. O.K.? Can you count furlong posts?"

I'd been about to protest that I couldn't possibly set the pace and I had no idea what a half-speed gallop was, but Alex's last mocking question stung me.

"Of course," I said, resolving to show him.

He drove off in the Land-Rover and we continued to walk round.

"How old is Mount Olive then?" I asked Geoff.

"Four-year-old," Geoff answered. "He broke down as a three-year-old. His owner's going to run him under National Hunt rules next season."

Jon, Jenny and Fred Wells were lining up, or rather walking in separate circles and then coming up into line.

"Now Jenny, get Darkie jumping off a bit brisker than you did last time," said Mr Phelps. "Are you all ready? Right, off you go."

They went, all jumping straight into a canter, a fast one too—at least it would have looked fast on Marsden Common. Watching Jon I didn't hear how the argument between Mark and Geoff began but as we walked round and Mr Phelps lined up the next three I caught snatches of insults and heard Geoff referring to "your friend Jimmy" in a very sneering voice. Then Mr Phelps came to tighten my girths and told them to stop nattering and ride round on the other rein.

When I rejoined them I asked Mark, "How fast is a half-speed gallop?"

"Mid way between a canter and a full speed gallop," he answered, "but I'll tell you when you're going fast enough. Keep a feel on his mouth when you push on."

80

I was just starting to say a grateful thank-you when Geoff butted in.

"Knows everything, does our Marky boy. He could teach the Guv'nor a thing or two about training and as for Les Cooper, well, he'd give him riding lessons if he got the chance. Knows how to stop a horse, too, Marky does, only he likes to keep his own hands clean so he gets silly little nits like Jimmy on the job—"

Mark's face was scarlet with rage and long before Geoff had finished his sentence he was trying to manœuvre High Jester alongside The Giant, then raising his whip he brought it down on Geoff's back with a tremendous crack. With a howl of rage and pain Geoff raised his to retaliate but a roar from Mr Phelps stopped him.

"If I have any more trouble from you two boys the Guv'nor's going to hear about it," he said and from the glare he gave them both I guessed he would have spoken much more ferociously if I hadn't been there.

"Now get lined up," he said.

Mount Olive seemed pleased at the prospect of a gallop. He pranced gently as we turned, I on the right, Mark on the left and Geoff in the centre. The Giant had his head up, fighting Geoff for the reins, High Jester plunged and then we were off. I supposed that this passed for a canter. Mount Olive's long stride gobbled up the ground at a fantastic rate, but he felt light and easy and I found to my relief that he was prepared to go the speed I asked. His perfect balance and the springy turf gave a wonderful sensation of lightness. I forgot the boys' quarrel, there was only wind and speed and Mount Olive now. We flashed past the first furlong post.

"Is this all right?" I shouted to Mark.

"Yes, you're doing fine," he shouted back.

I felt as though I was singing though actually I was saving my breath for the half-speed gallop; the second furlong post appeared and disappeared. Mount Olive was still moving effortlessly. I kept contact with his mouth and began to use my legs as we came to the third post. Mount Olive lengthened his stride and his body, his ears went further away, he leaned a little on my hands as he stretched into the gallop. It felt marvellous, the feeling of speed was intoxicating. I looked towards Mark and saw with misgiving that Geoff was edging The Giant closer to Jester. There was a frightening look of hatred in his eyes.

As he raised his whip I shouted to Mark to beware but it was too late, a galloping two-year-old isn't manœuvrable, and he was a sitting target as Geoff's whip came down across his hands. Mark gave a cry of pain, High Jester checked, swerved and almost fell. I began to slow up, but Mark quickly recovered, gathered up his reins and got Jester balanced again. We galloped on. Mark's face was furiously angry, he urged Jester on, drawing up on Geoff. Geoff sent The Giant on faster, we were really galloping now. Mount Olive stretched out even more, the ground came closer. The feeling of speed almost frightened me. I could see that Mark was still pursuing Geoff and gaining on him; The Giant was now at his top speed. Here was the fifth furlong post, we were supposed to slow down. I was the pace setter.

"Steady," I yelled at the boys. And I began to give and take with my hands. Mount Olive slowed his gallop but Jester and Giant forged ahead.

*"As he raised his whip I shouted to Mark to beware
but it was too late . . ."*

"Steady, slow up," I shouted at the boys but their quarrel seemed all that concerned them now. Mount Olive reduced his pace reluctantly and the gap between us widened as the boys rode on like demons. The two-year-olds were tiring, flagging, rolling a little in their gallop. They passed the Land-Rover, the group of horses and riders. I could hear furious shouts but I was only cantering now, I dropped my hands and Mount Olive slowed to a walk. Ahead I could see that the two-year-olds had come to an exhausted halt and the two boys had their whips out. But Alex's furious yells seemed to restore their senses. "What the hell do you mean by disobeying your riding orders?" he bellowed as he ran towards them. And "Are you mad, riding two-year-olds like that?" By then he was nearer to them than to us so we mercifully missed the rest.

I felt like bursting into tears, it had been so marvellous and so horrible at the same time. I wanted to join Jon but he was on a filly so I had to keep away. Cyril Redman came up to straighten Mount Olive's quarter sheet, and said that I'd be riding in the Newmarket Town Plate before I'd finished and then Jenny came up and said I'd better walk round.

When Alex had finished telling off the boys we rode back across the downs, an embarrassed and crestfallen party. Mark and Geoff were leading their tired horses and Alex Grant, announcing that they couldn't be trusted, sent Mr Phelps with us on Darkest Dawn and took Jenny in the Land-Rover. We rode home in dismal silence. I was glad when we reached the stables; it would have been a perfect morning if Geoff had left Mark in peace. I unsaddled and unbridled Mount

Olive and let him drink. Then I tried to get his head-collar on but he would look over his stable door to watch what was going on so I was still trying when Fred Wells appeared.

"Well, and what did you think of him?" he asked.

"Fabulous," I told him. "He's the best horse I've ever ridden and by far the fastest."

Fred Wells laughed. "Looked like a Derby finish as you came up to the five-furlong post. You should've heard the Guvnor's language. I don't know what's got into those boys." He tied Mount Olive up and began to groom him. I patted the red-gold neck and then I asked if there was anything I could do, but Fred said no, so I thanked him and went away across the yard to find Jon.

He'd been told to put a rug on Rosie and he'd just got it half on. "Here, come and give me a hand," he said in a low voice. "I've had three goes already. Do you think it matters if I don't get it there properly so long as it looks all right when it's on?"

When we'd got the rug on we retreated from the gloomy atmosphere of the stable yard to the kitchen. Mrs Hinde gave us jam tarts and lectured us on spoiling our lunches at the same time and then told us that Jimmy's mother had telephoned and there was still no sign of him at home. "Worried to death she is, poor soul, and not surprising. She says that he's not that sort of boy at all, not a bit adventurous."

"I think he's mixed up with Moonstruck, I don't care what anyone says," said Jon obstinately.

"Mark and Geoff seem to think so too," I said and told him more about their quarrel.

"They must have gone quite crazy to ride like that,"

said Jon, "though I must say it looked terrifically exciting; I'd have loved to be in your place. Alex was livid with rage, you should have heard his language. I don't blame him either, for as Fred Wells says, they could ruin two-year-olds riding like that and it's the trainer who has to face the owners."

Lunch was a very gloomy meal. Angela had evidently heard Geoff's side of the quarrel so she was furious with Mark and had had words with Katie, who stood up for him. Alex was as unapproachable as you would expect someone to be with his load of trouble.

As the meal ended Jon did something I would not have dared; he tackled Alex again on the subject of Jimmy.

"You remember you told us to pass on any information we picked up around the stable," he began. "Well, did you know that this quarrel between Mark and Geoff was mostly over Jimmy; they seem to think he was mixed up with Moonstruck in some way."

"Nonsense," said Alex. "Those boys are like a couple of jealous cats—they'll quarrel on any pretext or even without one. As for Jimmy, he's behaving like a spoilt child and he's going to find out that we don't want children in stables when he does turn up." With that he marched out leaving poor Jon very crestfallen.

Angela said, "Alex is in a foul mood. How I *hate* those beastly horses and that beastly stable," and her voice shook.

"Will you take me out riding?" asked Katie.

# CHAPTER SEVEN

### THE LETTER

ALEX didn't suggest that we exercised again on Saturday morning and neither Jon nor I had the courage to mention the matter. We stayed well away from the stables and arranged a handicap show jumping competition in the paddock. Katie had the jumps at one foot six and Jon and I at about three feet. We invited Angela to join in but she said that *she* hated competitions and *Goldie* hated show jumps.

Princess Amelia won. She jumped three clear rounds and I decided that although Mount Olive was the most wonderful horse I'd ever ridden, Princess Amelia was the one I would like to own. She had such a sweet nature as well as all her other accomplishments.

Though Alex hadn't a horse running he'd gone racing, so lunch was less gloomy and afterwards Mark appeared, looking rather excited.

"Try to shake off Katie," he muttered to me, "I want to talk to you two alone."

It wasn't so easy to shake off Katie for Angela had gone to Longbridge with Bert and his wife. But when we discovered that she had a friend in the village with whom she liked playing, I helped her to telephone and arrange for Emma to come over. With that settled, Jon and I went out to the saddle room where Mark was cleaning his tack.

Mark said, "Something very odd has happened. I don't know what to make of it. Look at this letter. Read the address on the envelope first."

The envelope was addressed to *Mrs. King, 15, Creek Street, Lewisham, London,* but that had been crossed out in pencil and *Mark Wilcox, Eastcombe Stables, near Longbridge,* had been added.

Jon was still studying the envelope when I whipped out the letter it contained. It was just a duty letter from Jimmy to his mother. He hadn't much to say: a bit about the horses. He was well, he hoped they all were. He'd be at home the weekend after next. It was the sort of letter everyone writes home when they can't think of anything suitable to tell their parents, but then, at the bottom, in the same stubby pencil that had re-addressed the envelope, was scrawled, *"I'm in a loft somewhere not far from Codling's stable. There's a pillarbox near and it's got a blue door. They won't let me out. Jimmy."*

We all looked at each other. I said, "It sounds unbelievable."

"Could it be a hoax?" asked Jon, studying the postmark.

"Could be," agreed Mark. "Anyone here could have picked up the letter, added the bits in pencil and posted it in the Ledhampton district."

"We'll have to investigate it," said Jon, obviously delighted at the thought.

"Have you shown it to anyone else," I asked Mark.

He shook his head. "I'm not popular at the moment, you're about the only people who will speak to me."

"Ought we to show it to Alex?" I asked.

*"No,"* answered Jon firmly. "He'll say it's nonsense and what's more he'll probably forbid us to investigate it. Where are Codling's stables, exactly, Mark?"

Mark drew a map of the downs in the dust on the saddle-room table. He drew our familiar range of downs and then another range, lying end to end. Beyond that was the village of Mossbury where Mr Codling had his stables.

"Their gallops are on Greely Down," he explained, "and a road runs here between the two sets of downs —they call it the Gap."

"How many miles?" asked Jon, pointing from Eastcombe to Mossbury.

And I asked, "Could we ride it?"

"Oh yes, I've ridden on Greely Down with Angela," answered Mark. "But if Geoff's behind the letter that's just what he wants—to see us setting off on a wild goose chase."

"Do we mind?" asked Jon. "He can laugh himself sick as far as I'm concerned."

"And we can't do nothing," I pointed out. "If there's any reason to suspect that Jimmy's being held prisoner."

"When can we go?" asked Jon. "Today? Tomorrow?"

"On the ponies it'll take us a couple of hours to get there, another two to come back and at least an hour to find the loft," said Mark gloomily. "Tomorrow's the only day I've got five hours free, but it's Sunday, the ponies are supposed to rest."

"Bicycles," suggested Jon, and I said, "Buses."

"You have to go into Longbridge to get the bus," Mark told us, "and most of them don't run on Sundays. We might be able to borrow a couple of bikes, but as I said, I'm out of favour and anyway most people want their own on Sundays. Then there's Jimmy, we've got to get him back and supposing we're pursued?"

"What do you think we should do then?" I asked.

"Well, if I had Goldie and we led Pincushion over for Jimmy we could make a quick getaway over the downs. But Angela's always on Geoff's side so I don't suppose she'll want to lend me the pony," Mark finished in depressed tones.

I couldn't resist a giggle at the thought of Jimmy making a quick getaway on the plump Pincushion, but Jon was taking it all very seriously.

"Shall Vivien and I go?" he asked. "We could go now, the ponies haven't done much today."

Mark shook his head. "Two's not enough," he said. "One of you would have to hold the ponies and that leaves only one to free Jimmy. Worse than useless."

"Well then, we must help ourselves to the ponies Sunday or not," said Jon.

"Oh Jon, we can't. They'll never forgive us," I said.

"It's a question of priorities," observed Jon. "We either offend the Grants or abandon Jimmy."

"If I was certain that it was a genuine letter I wouldn't hesitate," I said, "but supposing we take the ponies and then it turns out to be a hoax?"

"We'll have to explain," Jon answered. I could see us trying to explain that we'd been rescuing Jimmy from imaginary horse dopers to an enraged Alex. "We'll have to find out what they're doing then," I said. "We can't exactly snatch the ponies from under their noses and gallop down the drive."

"If we go before ten, Angela won't be up," Jon pointed out.

"We could tell Katie we were going to rescue Jimmy and swear her to secrecy," I said. "I'm sure she'd lend Pincushion then, but there's still Alex."

"He generally has a walk round the stables and then shuts himself up in his office. He always says he does the paper work on Sunday mornings," Mark told us. "As long as Mr Phelps doesn't think up any extra little jobs I should be through by ten, earlier if I get a move on. If you could take the four ponies down the road and wait for me on the track to the downs we'd be sure of getting away even if there was a hitch."

"Right, we'll do that," agreed Jon.

"And I'll think up something to tell Katie," I said.

The more we thought about it the more gloomy Jon and I became over the search for Jimmy. It was obviously one of those moments in life when you can't do the right thing by everyone. We hated the thought of abusing the Grants' hospitality but though we tried all day to think of a better plan, we couldn't, and when Sunday came, with a clear blue sky and bright sunshine, we knew that we would have to stick by our horrible choice.

We were up early and for once Bert was glad to accept our offer to muck out Chunky and Goldie. We were kept busy for we had four to groom as well and our breakfast to get. At nine-fifteen Jon went out to saddle and bridle and I rushed upstairs to square Katie who was still in bed. She was asleep so I wakened her very gently and then asked in my most persuasive manner, "Please, Katie, would you be very kind and lend us Pincushion? We've heard something about Jim, we may have found where he is, and if we led Pincushion over he could ride him back." As I feared Katie at once sat up and announced, "I'm coming too."

"But it's miles across the downs," I told her, "and we've got to ride fast. Besides if you come there won't be a pony for Jim to ride back. Please lend him, just this once."

"Oh, all right, I suppose I will," agreed Katie, rather disgruntled. "But you must promise to take me for a picnic ride and to have another jumping competition next week."

I promised and fled quickly before she could change her mind.

Alex was cooking his breakfast in the kitchen so we had to wait for him to finish and we hung about anxiously wondering where he was going to eat it. Both the sitting-room and the kitchen would be fatal to us as their windows would give him a full view of our departure, but mercifully he piled bacon, eggs, toast and coffee on a tray and took it to his office. Jon and I rushed to lead out our four ponies. Realising that we were frantic with haste the ponies immediately behaved like fiends. No sooner was Jon mounted than Pincushion reversed violently across the yard while Chunky marched resolutely forward. I hadn't even managed to mount. Every time I tried Goldie waltzed round Amelia entangling us in his reins so that one or the other of us was being half throttled. Jon, meanwhile, almost pulled out of the saddle by Pincushion, had let him go. My heart sank as with one leg through the reins, he set off at a brisk trot. I was quite sure Angela would appear at an upper window or Alex at the back door. However, Pincushion's one track mind led him straight to the saddle-room; he bolted in and finding the lid of the corn bin closed, plunged his head into a bag of pony nuts. I gave Jon Goldie to lead and hitching Amelia to the fence, went to retrieve Pincushion. He utterly refused to remove his head from the bag and went on guzzling nuts at a revolting speed. I tugged at his reins and cursed and finally walloped him one with my whip. He shot backwards, overturned the saddle-horse, and charged for the door, nuts dribbling from his mouth. I clung on to the reins and was dragged into the yard, battered by a collision with the doorpost but otherwise intact. But my wallop seemed to have done him good. He eyed me with a new respect, behaved while I mounted Amelia and moved forward in a docile manner.

As we increased the distance between us and the house, without a voice calling to ask where we were off to, so our spirits rose. It was a fine day and with an adventure before us and good ponies to ride it was easy to forget the possible outcome, easy not to think too far ahead. Anyway, I told myself, if we find Jimmy all will be forgiven.

Mark wasn't long in coming. We could hear his footsteps running down the road long before he appeared on the track to the downs; he was wearing jeans and carrying a parcel. "Packed lunch," he said breathlessly. "The Phelps have gone out for the day so we were each given one of these. Have you got anything? If not we may as well divide it up now, my pockets won't hold it all."

We stowed the food away and then with Mark on Goldie in the lead and Jon behind me ready to wallop

93

Pincushion if he went into reverse, we started on our journey.

Having a led horse spoiled it slightly for we could only go at the speed at which I could control my two. That meant no faster than a steady canter, which was frustrating when we were all itching for a flat-out gallop.

"Never mind, we'll make up for it coming back with Jim on Pincushion," said Jon, bursting with optimism. But when Mark looked at me to see if I felt as certain of success, we saw at once that we shared the same gnawing doubts.

We crossed our downs and descended by the chalky track where we'd caught High Jester; that adventure seemed to have happened an incredibly long time ago. We came to a small road and Mark, pointing to the narrow strip of flat land which wormed its way between the two stately ranges of down, said, "They call this the Gap."

It was a lonely road; one farmhouse and a pair of cottages which looked as though they stood always in the shade of one down or the other, were the only habitations you could see in any direction.

We left the road and took an uphill track. The day was growing hot, and climbing, the ponies began to sweat and over-fat Pincushion to flag. I cursed my anorak. We rode on and on and even Goldie became quite subdued. At last we reached the ridge of the next range of downs where magnificent views unfolded in every direction, but there was no time to admire them. Amelia, revived by the breeze which blew in fitful gusts, agreed to canter but the boys had to go behind to keep Pincushion going. I was sorry for him on his short little legs but at the same time I knew he was fat and idle, and this, after all, was a rescue operation not a pleasure trip.

The Codling gallops appeared; they seemed indistinguishable from the Eastcombe ones. I practised counting furlong posts until Pincushion's short legs could canter no further, then we slowed to a walk. Eventually the gallops ended and a meandering track led gently downhill. On the road there were huge notices *Racehorses—Dead slow*.

Mark took the lead. "We'd better ride straight past Codling's," he said. "Don't look too interested."

The stables were right beside the road so we had a good view of them over the brick wall and the white gate. The boxes, some brick, some timber, all with white doors, were built on three sides of a rectangle, the longest side facing the road. At the sound of our hoofs excitable thoroughbred heads appeared with wisps of hay dangling from their mouths.

"Well, this is Mossbury," announced Mark as we came to a cross-roads, "from now on your guesses are as good as mine. Any ideas?"

"It doesn't look exactly gigantic. I should think we'd better just ride round looking for the pillarbox and the blue door," said Jon.

"We could ask for the post office," I suggested, trying to save time and Pincushion's legs.

"If we see anyone," agreed Mark.

It wasn't a particularly pretty village; there were a few ancient cottages and some rather horrible Victorian ones. We went straight over the cross-roads catching a glimpse of a pub, the White Hart, one way and a church the other. The village ended almost at once.

We were enclosed by hedges just bursting into leaf and beyond were smooth fields, some rich brown and newly sown, others green with sprouting crops. We rode on and on. There were no habitations in sight, much less lofts with blue doors.

"Let's go back and try another road," suggested Jon. "This one's a dead loss."

"I wonder what he means by 'near'?" I said.

"It would depend on how he was taken there," answered Mark. "I mean two miles is nothing in a car, but on your feet—"

"That means another ten minutes," grumbled Jon. "If we're riding at six miles an hour and we've got to search two miles. What a bore; I do hate roadwork."

We rode deeper and deeper into the country. The frustratingly empty fields enfolded us in a silence only broken by peewits and the distant drone of a tractor.

Just as Jon's ten minutes were coming to an end, we saw a postbox ahead and all our hearts leapt with excitement until we reminded each other that this wasn't the pillarbox Jim had noticed, but a tiny postbox.

"Still, he would have been in a fuss when he wrote that letter," Jon pointed out. "He might easily have written pillarbox by mistake."

"Easily," I agreed, pulling up, for there was a lane beside the box and a signpost saying 'Daggit's Farm'. We stood in our stirrups looking for lofts, but the lane was too long for us to get a good view of the farm buildings and there could be dozens of blue doors concealed behind the huge Dutch barn. We turned down the lane.

"What are we going to say?" asked Jon.

"Have you a loft with a blue door?" I answered and giggled.

"Does Mr Jeremy Tree live here?" suggested Mark.

"Why Jeremy Tree?" asked Jon.

"Because he isn't likely to, the odds are against it," said Mark. "Ten to one he's Tom Smith."

"We could say we were on a treasure hunt and we had to find a loft with a blue door near a pillarbox," I suggested.

"We could," said Jon doubtfully.

"It depends on the person. He might help or he might think we were wasting his time with silly games," said Mark.

We reached Daggit's still undecided, but the giant cattle sheds and grain-driers and Dutch barns had no human life so when we had made sure there was nothing remotely resembling a loft with a blue door, we hurried away.

"Back to Mossbury?" asked Jon.

The ponies were delighted, they thought they were going home. I realised that it was lunch time and that I was starving.

"If we could find the post office it might be open and selling ice cream," I suggested.

"But you're sharing my food," said Mark. "It's communal since you helped carry it."

"Communal and squashed, I should think," observed Jon.

We returned to the cross-roads in Mossbury and found the post office two doors from the White Hart. It was just a room in a cottage and it was closed. And there was no loft with a blue door anywhere near; Jon and I trailed up and down the road looking while

Mark was in the pub buying soft drinks and crisps. Then we rode on again until we came to a field with a water trough just outside the village. We watered the ponies and grazed them on a grassy bank while we ate. Mark kept hurrying us and the moment the last mouthful was eaten he was tightening Goldie's girths.

"I think we'd better divide to search the last two roads," he said. "Otherwise we won't be through in time. If you'll do this one together I'll go down by the church."

I was just going to argue and say it would be more fun to stick together when I remembered that Mark had a deadline, he had to be back for evening stables and here we were slowing things up with trivial chatter.

"Right," I agreed, stuffing sandwich paper and crisp bags into my pockets and then trying to organise my two ponies. "Twenty minutes?" asked Jon.

"Fifteen there, fifteen back," said Mark. "We can trot on a bit now they've had a rest. And if we find it, we'll come straight back to the cross-roads and wait for the others."

It was a lovely afternoon and growing warmer every minute. I cursed my anorak and Jimmy, for after-lunch lethargy made me long to lie lazily on a grassy bank instead of dragging Pincushion along a hot, dull, loft-less road with Chunky neighing deafeningly for Goldie.

We met a girl of about sixteen on a bicycle and I asked her if there was a pillarbox anywhere ahead. But, dismounting from her bicycle, she said the nearest one was in Mossbury and gave us long and careful directions. We thanked her and trotted on. When at long last our fifteen minutes were up we turned back with an equal lack of enthusiasm. Somehow I'd quite given up expecting to find Jimmy. I was resigned to the fact that the letter was a hoax, to returning to East-combe to find Geoff, Brian and Sandy roaring with laughter while Alex and Angela seared us with angry sarcasm. All that mattered now was to get back so that Mark wouldn't be late for evening stables.

Resigned to failure it took me some time to realise that Mark, waiting at the cross-roads, was trying to hurry us with excited waves of his hand, and Jon, busy controlling Chunky, didn't notice either.

"Come on," said Mark, setting off at a trot the moment we reached him. "It isn't a pillarbox, not a real round one, but a postbox in a wall, but the loft's there *and* it has a blue door."

"How far?" asked Jon.

"About two miles. But there's a grass verge most of the way."

It seemed more like three to me and to Pincushion it obviously seemed about twenty miles. I don't think he'd ever gone so far or so fast in his life before. We were in very unpopulated country when Mark said, "Slow up, we're almost there." Mark pointed silently to a postbox in a wall and turned down a lane at a left angle to the road. On the corner, facing the lane, was a hideous red-brick house with yellow tile decorations round its tall, narrow windows. And behind the house was a well-built brick building with a loft above. Both the double door below and the loft door above were painted blue! The whole place had a slightly derelict air and beyond the house was one of those depressing fields studded with pig sheds and rooted brown by pigs.

We rode briskly past. I was looking at the loft, searching for a window at which Jimmy's pale face might appear at the sound of our hoofs, but there was only the door in front and the eaves came too low for side windows.

Some way down the lane Mark stopped. "Did you see the old man in the yard sawing wood?" he asked. "We can't just walk in."

We let the ponies graze while we tried to decide on a plan of action.

"Sunday afternoon," said Mark despondently. "He may saw until tea-time."

"Not much on television," agreed Jon.

"We could cross the pig field and approach from the back," I suggested.

"We'll have to do something, and quickly," said Mark with a desperate look at his watch.

"You could go back now we've found it," I suggested. "And Jon and I could just wait here until the old man goes out."

"And supposing he doesn't?" asked Mark. "If Jimmy really is imprisoned there they wouldn't hesitate to lock up another of us and you'd be easy game, one trying to get to Jimmy and the other holding three ponies."

"It's probably just a hoax," said Jon.

I was just going to point out that now the blue door existed Jimmy must be behind it when I realised that it would be funniest of all to send us on a chase to a real place and then land us in some terrible misunderstanding with the owner. "Well, I think we should make a dash across the pig field and then, if there's no sign of Jimmy we should go home," I said, firmly.

"Come on, Jon, she's right," said Mark, sliding off Goldie and handing me his reins.

"Here, have I got to hold all these beastly ponies?" I demanded.

Mark said, "Yes," and Jon made a triumphant face and said, "This is *man's* work." They stepped over the link fencing and began to run diagonally across the field. I was hoping that they had thought of something sensible to say if they were caught and that there was no one looking out of an upstair window of the house. Soon they had completely disappeared. I listened for angry shouts and wondered what I would do if they were captured. I had visions of trying to dial 999 with Pincushion in reverse, Goldie galloping for home and Chunky in the telephone kiosk. As the moments passed and nothing happened I began to visualise Geoff and Brian and Sandy watching the drama from the loft, killing themselves with laughter and probably with a hose at the ready waiting to soak Jimmy's would-be rescuers.

Suddenly the boys reappeared. They were running fast but with caution. I tried to straighten the ponies into an orderly line, ready for a quick getaway, but Jon and Mark slowed up as they drew near. I could see by their faces that they were very excited.

"He *is* there," said Jon, "*and* he saw us."

"Shush, don't yell," objected Mark.

"You didn't speak to him?" I asked.

"He was at the window," Mark explained. "It was small and very dirty so we couldn't see him plainly but he waved like mad when he saw us."

"You couldn't get him out?"

"Not a hope without a ladder and it would be a job then. The window's very small and there's no sill or anything to rest on," answered Mark.

"We'll have to rush it from the front," said Jon, "as soon as the old man stops sawing."

"But the door's obviously locked," I objected.

"We'll batter it down," said Jon. "It doesn't look all that strong."

"Well, what do we do now?" I asked.

"Keep watch," Jon answered.

"And we can't see him from here."

"We'll have to wander up and down the lane without raising suspicion," said Mark. "You could pick flowers but I don't know what Jon and I could do; it's too early for blackberries."

"Catch butterflies," suggested Jon, making a graceful leap with an imaginary net and nearly frightening Goldie out of his wits.

I gave him Pincushion to hold and handed Amelia's reins to Mark. I was tired of horse holding. I began to pick flowers to make a decent bunch before I reached the house so that my occupation would be obvious. But the chief flower was wild parsley so I decided that I would gather food for a rabbit rather than plucking a few choice blooms for some fiddly flower arrangement.

The old man was still sawing; he obviously meant to be warm next winter. His hair was white, his face red and quite aggressive looking. He wasn't large but on the other hand he didn't look as doddery as I had hoped. I wondered if two of us would be a match for him if it came to a stand-up fight.

I wandered about the entrance to the lane until I had collected enough greenery for at least ten rabbits, then I returned with the dreary news that the old man was still sawing with undiminished energy.

"Still sawing?" asked Mark as I shared out my rabbit food among the ponies.

We waited for as long as we could bear and then Jon, wearing a village-idiot smile—he said he was admiring the beauties of nature—strolled down the lane.

Mark looked at his watch. His expression was one of desperate resignation. I suppose that he was thinking of his burned boats, for now there was no chance of reaching Eastcombe by four.

I tried to think of something to talk about, something to keep our minds off the future so I asked Mark where he had learned to ride and we got on the subject of riding schools. We were talking about our first gymkhanas when Jon came back.

"He's stopped sawing. He's pottering about doing other jobs," Jon told us. "He filled a water bucket and now he's sweeping up in the barn place below the loft; I think he may have a horse in there."

"Perhaps he'll want his tea soon," said Mark hopefully. "Sawing is thirsty work."

"So is pony holding," I remarked, battling with Pincushion who was again dissatisfied with his grazing ground.

We waited and then Mark, looking less horsey in jeans than Jon and me in jodhpurs, walked briskly down the lane. It was ages before he came back, rather shaken and out of breath. "He made tea and took a mug and a plate with a bun on it up to the loft," Mark told us. "I thought I'd rush him and with Jimmy's help we'd have a good chance of overpowering him; it all happened so suddenly there was no time to fetch Jon. I crept into the yard and was really close to him when he was standing on the ladder. But then, instead of unlocking the door he pushed open one of those cat doors at the bottom and shoved the tea in. I ran. I think I just got clear before he turned round; anyway he didn't shout after me."

"And what's he doing now?" asked Jon.

"Indoors having his own tea. I think we'll have to move in now, because it may be that the old man is only holding the fort."

"You mean he may be Grandfather and Mum and Dad and two large sons will all come back any minute?" I asked.

"Exactly," said Mark. "Come on, Jon."

"It's my turn to keep watch," I protested, but saying that I was no use at fighting, Jon flung me two pairs of reins and ran after Mark. I persuaded the ponies there was better grass down the lane, nearer the house. I wanted to know what was going on and besides it was obviously no use having the transport too far from our escape route. I hadn't gone far when the boys came hurrying back.

"He's already finished his tea," said Jon, "and he's mixing stuff in buckets."

"We think he's going to feed the pigs," added Mark. "They're all grunting at the gate, so we'd better get out of sight right up the lane where the hedge begins."

The ponies, even Princess Amelia, assumed disgruntled expressions at this further example of pointless behaviour though when they reached the hedge-

sheltered place they were pleased with the new grass.
Through the thick screen of overgrown quickthorn we
watched the old man emptying buckets of food into
two troughs by the pig-field gate. Then he disappeared towards the house again and I set off to keep
watch. I couldn't think of anything more original than
collecting another meal for my rabbits and I found a
good patch of dandelions quite close to the house and
loft. There was no sign of the old man. I picked
slowly, choosing only the choicest leaves. Then, suddenly, the old man marched out of the front door, no
longer in his shirt sleeves but wearing a tie and jacket.
He stepped into the lane, shut the gate behind him and
walked towards the road. I waited, barely able to
control my excitement; he might only be going to the
postbox, but he went past it, and I heard his footsteps
go on along the road.

· I dropped my armful of greenery and tore up the
lane to the boys.

## CHAPTER EIGHT

### SEEING DOUBLE

"HE's gone out," I called breathlessly before I even
reached the boys, "Quick!" I grabbed Amelia and
Pincushion and hurried them down the lane.

"Are you sure?" Jon asked. "It may be just to post
a letter."

"No, he's gone past the box and he's put on a jacket

and tie." I hitched Pincushion to one yard gatepost and Amelia to the other. I was determined not to be left miles from the scene of action pony-holding. Mark found a ring in the wall and tied Goldie to it, Jon slung Chunky's reins over the garden gate. Mark was first up the loft steps, he slid back the cat entrance and yelled, "Jim," then he began to kick the door; it was a stout one and he merely dented the paint.

"Ask Jim if he knows where they keep the key," I suggested.

Jon, another believer in brute force, had found a heavy log waiting for the saw and was proposing to use it as a battering ram.

"He says the younger man's gone out for the day and taken the key with him," Mark called.

That meant a doubling of danger; two strong men would certainly overpower two of us. We must be *quick*, so while the boys were both on the loft steps, trying to balance themselves so that they could swing Jon's log at the door, I ran round to the back of the building. The window, as they had said, was small and high. I stood looking at it helplessly. It was terrible to have found Jimmy, then not to be able to free him. Suddenly I remembered that lofts had their own links with loose-boxes. I'd read—was it in Black Beauty?— of a stable boy shaking the hay through a hole in the loft floor directly into the hayrack below. But were there still stables below?

There was a side door into the building as well as the double door at the end. Inside it was almost dark, the two windows looking across the pig field were thickly draped with cobwebs, but a grey horse munched in one loose-box and the other was filled with a tidy

"*The boys were still battering but they seemed to have had little effect.*"

stack of logs, hay, straw, a cornbin and a large number of empty bottles. The logs were stacked beside the manger, beneath the old-fashioned iron hayrack. I climbed up and tugged frantically at the bars of the hayrack; nothing yielded. I went into the coachhouse or cart-shed part of the building. It was fitted out as a workshop; a wooden bench, rows and rows of tools. I opened a small door set in one of the double doors and emerged into the yard. The boys were still battering, but apart from destroying the paint, they seemed to have had little effect. They looked hot and desperate. The ponies were still there though Chunky was systematically destroying a rose bush.

I said, "Ask Jimmy about the hayracks. Is there a way through, a hole into each of them from the loft or have they been blocked up?"

Mark asked and then passed on Jimmy's answer. "There are trap doors. He climbed down into one rack but the bars are solid iron and wouldn't give an inch. Do you think we could get him out that way?"

"Well, there are plenty of tools in here." The boys dropped their battering-ram and hurried into the barn. I grabbed a huge hammer and ran back to the loose-box. I climbed up on the log stack. Jimmy's white face glimmered above me. Mark had a crowbar, he stood on the manger and prised while I hammered.

Jon was still inspecting the tools with exasperating slowness but suddenly between my ringing bashes I heard a joyful cry of, "I've found a hacksaw."

He pushed Mark aside and began to saw at the stout iron bars. To my amazement it worked. "Cuts like cheese," shouted Jon in a voice of triumph. "Won't take long now, Jim!"

108

But though he worked fast a good many bars would have to be cut through to make a hole large enough for Jimmy. Four at least, top and bottom, I reckoned. It was agony waiting. If only he doesn't wreck the saw, I thought. Supposing it blunted? Supposing Jimmy's gaolers returned? I ran through the coach-house. The ponies were still there. Chunky had up-rooted a shrub, there was no sign of the old man. I ran back. Jon had just dropped the second bar, but the hole still looked desperately narrow.

Mark grabbed my arm. "Look in here," he said and his voice was full of suppressed excitement. He pulled me into the other loose box. The grey horse I'd barely glanced at was a lovely thoroughbred filly—she looked to me like a racehorse and very out of place in that dark stable.

"Don't you recognise her?" asked Mark. "It's Moonstruck."

"But how did she get *here*?" I asked quietly so's not to distract Jon.

"They must have stolen her after we left this morning. We'll have to take her with us. Could you ride Goldie? Then I could lead her from Amelia," he asked, taking a head-collar from a pail in the wall.

"Yes," I was prepared to agree to anything so long as we all got out quickly. I went back to help Jon. He was on his fourth bar.

"Ready, Jim?" he called. "Come down feet first and we'll guide you down on to the log stack."

The fourth bar fell and Jimmy's feet swung through the hole. He didn't like trusting his weight to us. "It's too small, I'm sticking," he wailed.

"Let go, put your arms by your sides," directed Jon.

"I can't," cried Jimmy, scrabbling desperately at the floor above.

Mark was leading Moonstruck out. "Footsteps on the road," he called.

Jimmy let go. There was a sound of tearing shirt as we pulled him through. He stood dazed.

"Run," I shrieked at him. "Pincushion's outside," and we ran to the ponies.

I untied Goldie. Mark's beastly short stirrups made mounting a struggle but from the lane Jon called, "Hurry, he's coming," and I was on. Jon was on, too, and was trying to help Jimmy so I went to Mark's aid, for Moonstruck was refusing to lead. One smack on her rump and we surged into the lane. Jimmy mounted at last but the saddle was slipping slowly and inexorably round Pincushion's fat stomach.

"Hang on," we yelled at him, for up the lane came the old man, a package under his arm.

Jimmy, perched on nylon girth with saddle under one leg, swayed horribly but clung on to Pincushion's mane. The old man shouted and tried to bar the lane with outstretched arms, but we charged and he was almost knocked down by Chunky as we swept past and out into the road. We tore along at a tremendous trot, Jimmy clinging on white-faced until Jon called, "He isn't following." Then we stopped and I jumped off to help Jimmy while Mark sorted out Moonstruck and Jon kept watch.

"He could be telephoning friends in the village to stop us," said Mark as we set off again. "So keep close together."

We approached the cross-roads in a solid block, but

there was no one to bar our passage. The next danger point was Codling's stables, but evening stables were evidently over and no one rushed out at the urgent hammer of our hoofs. As we saw the downland track also unguarded we all gave great sighs of relief and slowed up. I let down Mark's left-over stirrups and fear gave way to triumph. We've done it, I thought, we've rescued Jimmy.

Jon was still looking back anxiously and Mark said, "They'd soon catch up with us in a Land-Rover so we'd better keep going."

We kept going, riding into the cool evening with the sun setting behind us until the boys decided we could walk. Then Jimmy began his story.

"Well, you see, I thought I'd do a bit of investigation on my own so I went to see Alan Fane, he's one of Codling's lads, but he comes from Lewisham same as I do. Went to my school and it was 'cause he went into stables that I decided to. I caught the 'bus there on the Saturday, you see, and went in and asked for Al but they said he wasn't there, he'd left. So back I went to the 'bus stop and then a car stopped and this man asked me if I would like a hitch into Longbridge. Then he started asking me questions, was I looking for Alan? Wasn't I one of Grant's lads? And he drove me round to that house and when I started to kick up he and the old man bundled me up into the loft."

"But how did you send the letter?" I asked. "We'd never have known where to look but for that."

"Well, you see, I'd been carrying round this letter for my Mum forgetting to post it and first I thought I'd add a bit about what had happened and try to get it to her, but then I thought, she won't know what to do and my stepfather'll say I'm just messing about, so I decided to send it to Mark."

"But how did you post it?" asked Jon.

"Well, you see, there was this little girl, younger than Katie, but she had started school, about five I suppose. She was always posting things through that cat-hole in the loft door. You know, sweets and kid's books and pictures she'd drawn and even a teddy bear to keep me company. I asked her if she could really post letters and she said she could so I gave it to her. She said she could reach the box, she stood on the bank or something, but I wasn't sure that she'd really done it."

When Jim had finished his story I let the jogging Goldie go his twenty yards ahead and as he walked into the dusk with a long stride and an outstretched neck I began to enjoy riding him. But not for long; suddenly there was a shout from behind. I turned expecting pursuers and saw that the others had stopped, Mark had dismounted and was feeling Moonstruck's foreleg.

"She's gone lame," Jon explained.

"Absolutely hopping lame," added Mark in a harassed voice. "I'm afraid she's broken down. There's nothing in her foot and her tendon's up." I could see that he was blaming himself for the wild riding through Mossbury.

"She didn't just tread on something?" I suggested.

"No, look," he led her forward and even at the walk she was painfully lame. My heart sank. We stood round looking at her and wondering what on earth to do now. Mark spoke first. "If you all went on and told them at the stables they could send a box for her. I think she'll just make the Gap road; it's not far now and we can take it very slowly."

"But we can't just leave you on your own," I objected. "Anything might happen."

"We must divide into two parties," said Jon. "And if we put Jimmy in one and Moonstruck in the other we'll have *some* evidence as long as one gets home."

"Yes, all right then, Jimmy and Vivien go on," agreed Mark. "You and I are the best if it comes to a stand-up fight, Jon."

"But I don't want to leave you two in the worst danger," I objected.

"You've still got to get across the Gap," Mark pointed out. "If they're waiting there you'll have to gallop for it. Stick to Vivien's tail, Jim, and don't let them get you again."

Jimmy's face was white and anxious in the dusk and I thought I could hear his teeth chattering.

"We'll charge them," I said, "and no human frame could stand up to Pincushion heading for home and supper."

"You'd better tell the horsebox to give three hoots," said Mark, "then we'll know it's them and not the old man waiting for us."

We galloped the last stretch of Greely Down, but when we reached the track down to the Gap road we rode very cautiously and spoke only in whispers. I was wondering what I would do to hold up a party of horses and riders and had just come to the conclusion that I'd use a car or something to block most of the track when Jim whispered, "Look there's a car!" There, round the next bend a cream-coloured car stood between us and the road. I stopped Goldie dead, but Pincushion marched on; intent on the prospects of supper he ignored Jim's aids and even a great haul on his mouth. Feeling much more like fleeing back to the down I trotted after them, trying to grab a rein. But Pincushion wasn't having that, he put down his head, broke into a canter and gaining momentum bore down on the parked car. Unable to think of an alternative, I followed. I was expecting men with evil faces to stretch out grasping hands for my reins, but instead as we swept by there was a shrill scream and I caught a glimpse of a girl and a man, their arms round each other, sitting in the car. Pincushion had increased his speed; Jim seemed to have abandoned all hope of stopping him and was holding on to the mane. The road loomed ahead. I must slow up, I thought, I couldn't risk bringing Goldie down on the road; so as Pincushion met the tarmac with a horrible metallic screech of sliding shoes, I steadied to a trot. Jimmy was still in the saddle and Pincushion was making for the homeward track. I reached the road just as there was a sudden roar of an accelerating engine and a car, headlights blazing, came hurtling along the road straight at me. I dithered—backwards or forwards?

"It's them," yelled Jimmy.

Goldie had taken charge; he leapt rather than galloped across the road and for a horrible moment I thought we and the car were bound to collide, but with an anguished scream of brakes it swerved and, as we galloped up the track in pursuit of Pincushion, I caught a glimpse of it slewed round, half on the verge.

"I hope they're in the ditch for good," shouted Jimmy. "That was the car they picked me up in, blue

Austin. They'll be searching the track for Moonstruck now. Good thing really we had to leave her behind."

As soon as we were on familiar ground our spirits began to rise and the nearer we drew to Eastcombe the more Jimmy talked. I suppose he was making up for his days of silence in the loft. I couldn't hear half he said because Goldie insisted on being yards ahead, but when we came off the gallops and took the track home he at last consented to walk, even with Pincushion jogging on his tail.

"It's a good job Mark thought of bringing Moonstruck," Jim was saying. "She's proof, you see. Otherwise it would have been just my word against theirs and the police might have thought I was making it up or something. I'll have something to tell my Mum, won't I? Not that my stepfather will believe it, he doesn't think much of me really. Partly on account of my size, he's a big man you see."

"Well, that was a brilliant idea of yours to send the letter," I told him. I didn't feel much like conversation. Now we were out of danger and almost home I'd begun to worry over Mark and Jon. The men would obviously continue to wait at the bottom of the track for Moonstruck to appear or they would search the track itself, for they must realise that we would send help as soon as we reached home. And what hope would the boys have of escape with Moonstruck dead lame? I knew that Mark would refuse to leave her. It was all a question of time, I thought, urging Goldie into a trot, we must get the box there quickly.

It was quite dark now, except that if you've been out in it a long time the dark is never as dark as all that. There were no lights on in the house so I followed

115

Jimmy, who had already opened the yard gate and was calling, "Mr Phelps."

Eighteen excited heads appeared over their loose-box doors. I looked round. Yes, all the usual boxes were full and the grey face next to High Jester was undeniably Moonstruck's.

The total horror of the situation hit me. "Jim, she's there," I heard myself wail. "That other grey—"

Jim looked at me helplessly. "We can't send the box," I said. "We'll have to go back and tell them. We'll have to take her home." We'd stolen a horse and lamed it. I felt terrible as I visualised Mark and Jon encouraging those slow painful steps across the downs bringing her, as they thought, home to safety.

"Come on, quickly," I told Jimmy. I turned the reluctant Goldie and set off down the drive. He swerved towards his stable, protesting that the day had been long enough already, but I forced him on. Sorry as I felt for him we had to go back and tell the boys the terrible news.

Behind me Jimmy battled with Pincushion, overcame him and clattered out on the road.

Suddenly there were shouts from behind us and running feet. We couldn't stop for explanations now. Feeling like a criminal I tore down the road. We were almost at the track to the downs when a Land-Rover came round the corner from the village and stopped abruptly. The Grants, Alex, Angela, and Katie jumped out and barred our way.

"What the *hell* is going on?" asked Alex. "We've been searching the countryside for you. I see you've found Jimmy, but where are Jon and Mark?"

"They're still on the downs," I said, "we must go back and find them."

"Oh, no, you don't," said Alex, taking a firm hold of Goldie's reins. "And what have you got to say for yourself, Jimmy King?"

Jimmy looked at him helplessly, not knowing where to begin, and then burst into tears.

"Oh, hell," said Alex in a disgusted voice. "Come on, get off these poor wretched ponies. Brian and Sandy, will you take them up and put them away. There's water and hay ready and Bert'll feed them later."

We were pushed into the Land-Rover, driven to the house and marched indoors. All the time Jimmy was sobbing noisily and my mind was in a hopeless turmoil. What could I do? The boys on the down, the lame horse, the lurking men and the dark, it added up to an impossible situation. We'd stolen a horse and wrecked it and there seemed no way at all of putting things right. Suddenly and unexpectedly I began to cry too.

"Oh, *no*," said Alex. "Look, Angela, we'd better feed them. You scramble some eggs. Into the kitchen everyone and Katie, try and find the box of tissues. Jimmy has no handkerchief and the dirtiest hands I've ever seen."

We sat at the kitchen table and I tried to stop the silly flow of tears. Alex waited a minute or two and then he said, "Vivien, you're older and you've only been missing for eight hours. Would you mind pulling yourself together and telling me what has happened?"

The smell of scrambling eggs and toasting bread was reassuring and made the world of the dark downs and

117

stolen horses seem the unreal one. I mopped and sniffed and tried to think where to begin.

"We went to look for Jimmy," I began. "He'd sent this peculiar letter to Mark and though we thought it might be a hoax we decided we must make sure so we went over to Mossbury to look for the pillarbox and the loft with the blue door.

"What loft?" cried Angela. But Alex said, "Shush, details later."

"There was an old man on guard," I went on, "but the boys got round to the back and saw Jimmy at the window. We kept watch all day waiting for the old man to go out and when he went we tried to break down the door but it was too strong, so we found a hacksaw and Jon sawed up a hayrack and we pulled Jimmy through."

"Ripped my shirt to pieces," sobbed Jimmy.

"And then we found the horse. A grey filly, we thought it was Moonstruck—" my voice trailed away, this was the worst part of the story, but it had to be told. I nerved myself to go on. "We all thought it was Moonstruck and that they must have stolen her since we left this morning, so we took her too. The old man tried to stop us, but we got away to the downs and then half-way across Greely she went dead lame. And we've left Jon and Mark there with her and they still think she's Moonstruck." I began to cry again. Angela plonked a plate of scrambled eggs in front of me and Alex said, "A grey filly exactly like Moonstruck. This interests me exceedingly. Go on." It was so unexpected, when I'd been waiting for a roar of rage that I went on.

"The car which kidnapped Jimmy was waiting for

us on the road through the Gap, it charged me and skidded and that's all really except that the boys are on the down and the men are waiting for them on the Gap road and it's dark."

"Well, dark never killed anyone," said Alex briskly. "Where was this loft?"

"Two or three miles outside Mossbury," I answered. "If you're coming from Codling's you turn right and go down the road beside the church."

"And Jimmy was kidnapped?"

"Yes, he went to Codling's to ask a friend about Moonstruck and afterwards a man offered him a lift."

Jimmy, who's been eating eggs heavily salted with tears put down his knife and fork. "He drove me to this house instead of into Longbridge and when I began to create they set on me and dragged me up into the loft and there I was locked in for days and days," with that he pushed away his plate and sobbed inconsolably.

"This sounds like a job for the police as well as the Stewards," said Alex Grant. "Vivien, tell me again, where exactly are the boys?" I told him and that the horsebox was to hoot three times, and he went off to the office.

I ate. I didn't feel hungry, only weak and empty. Katie looked anxiously at Jimmy. "They kept you locked up all that time," she said. "They must be really horrible men."

And Angela said, "You Bradleys do look for trouble, don't you?" And, "Would you like some ice cream? There's lots."

Jimmy and I were both eating ice cream when Alex came back. "A police car and the horsebox are on their way," he said, "and if you two will wash your faces we'll go round in the Land-Rover and join them."

"Me, too?" asked Katie.

"Yes, we can't leave you in an empty house."

As we drove round the downs and through Upton Greely Alex asked Jimmy about Alan Fane. Jimmy explained about being at the same school.

"And did he do Moonstruck?" asked Alex.

"Not that I know of," Jimmy answered, "but I thought he might be able to tell me something that would help to get Mark out of trouble."

When we came to the Gap the police car and the horsebox were there already and Mark and Jon, lit by the headlamps, stood in the midst of the group in the road. Practically all the staff from Eastcombe had come in the box and they were exclaiming over the extraordinary likeness which the grey filly bore to Moonstruck while Mark, looking stunned, refused to believe that Moonstruck was safe at home.

I went to pat Amelia and tell her that her horrible day was almost over. She and Chunky rushed into the horsebox the moment the ramp was lowered; they were obviously delighted to save themselves those last few miles, and the grey filly hobbled up after them.

The police had been talking to Alex and as soon as the box had driven away we set off for Mossbury; Jon and Mark in the police car, the rest of us following in the Land-Rover.

The whole adventure had suddenly become unreal to me and I had a horrible feeling that the red-brick house with the yellow tile decorations and the loft didn't really exist and that we wouldn't be able to show them to the police. But they were there all right.

Chunky's uprooted shrub lay beside the garden gate and the paint on the loft door bore the marks of the boys' battering ram.

The police rang the bell but there was no answer so they took Jimmy to show them the stable and the hay-rack, and Alex went along too. Meanwhile I told Mark and Jon about the loving couple and the car charging me at the Gap and asked whether they had had any trouble.

They hadn't; Mark said he supposed they'd come so slowly that the kidnappers thought they'd gone an-other way; there were other ways. And Jon said we should have got the loving couple to help us, but I pointed out that Pincushion hadn't given us a chance.

Katie said she hoped Pincushion's legs would be all right after so much work, and when would we take her for a picnic ride?

When the police inspection was over we all packed into the cars again, only this time Jimmy and I were with the police. They were very friendly but they weren't terribly interested in me; they asked Jimmy about Alan Fane and what his address was. Then they made him describe the kidnapping in terrific detail—exactly who had brought him food and things like that.

Back at the house we all found we were starving so a positive feast took place. Jimmy ate five sausages, while Mark and Jon had bacon and eggs, half a beef-steak pie and bread and cheese all at once. Angela said that she thought Mrs Hinde would be quite pleased, she was always grumbling about the leftovers, and hotted up some stew for anyone who had any room. Alex came in from the stables; he had inspected our ponies as well as the grey filly, and started a second supper of cold meat and salad, while Katie consumed a large bowl of cereal and I ate sardines, stew and apples.

Presently Mark and Jimmy were sent off to the Phelps' and Jon, Katie and I were told to go to bed. Angela said very firmly that she hadn't had an exhausting day and was going to tie-dye some clothes.

I had a bath; Jon, disgusting as ever, said he didn't need one, so he gave Katie an exact account of the day as her good-night story.

When I wakened on Monday morning my watch had stopped but since it was full daylight I went to wake Jon. His watch had stopped too. Angela's and Katie's empty rooms and thumping noises downstairs told me that it was late so I dragged on clean jeans and a yellow sweater and went down.

Mrs Hinde didn't give me her usual lecture on sloth. She said, "The kettle's on for coffee, dear, and you did have a day yesterday by all accounts." And then she asked, "Is Jon awake? The police are coming at twelve and Mr Grant asked me to see you were both up by then." I yelled the information about the police up the stairs to Jon and then got on with my breakfast. Mrs Hinde bustled round grumbling about Angela.

"Do you know what the daft girl did last night? Dyed all her clothes emerald green. You should see them out there, a line full. Practically every stitch she's got, underwear and all. Emerald green underwear indeed—I wouldn't have it if she were my daughter."

The police, who arrived punctually at twelve, were plain-clothes detectives and they brought a boy with them. Short, with fair curly hair, he looked twelve

122

from behind and seventeen when you saw his face so we guessed he was an apprentice. When we reached the yard Jimmy, looking incredibly clean—I think Mrs Phelps had been scrubbing him—rushed up with a cry of "Alan" and the rest of the stable staff downed their grooming tools and came out into the yard. Alex and Mr Phelps talked earnestly to the detectives and Mark stood by his boxes, only now instead of High Jester two grey heads looked out side by side.

"Well, let's make the test before it melts," said one of the detectives and grinning broadly Alan Fane opened the paper bag he was carrying and drew out an ice-cream cornet.

"I did Swan's Mist at Codling's," he explained, "and she ate ices. There are other ways of telling them apart but when people played the fool, you know how they do in stables, and tried to muddle me up, I'd run to the post office for an ice cream and that settled it, for Moonstruck never touched them."

"Well, this is the lame filly, the one we found at Mossbury," said Mark, and Alan offered her the ice, but already a greedy grey nose from next door was stretched out trying to grab it. Alan pointed to our Moonstruck and said, "That's Swan's Mist and she's never won a race in her life."

Of course then the whole mysterious business became clear. Mr Sinclair had two grey fillies and when the really good Moonstruck went lame, or 'broke down' as they say in racing circles, he decided to run the dud Swan's Mist in her name. He knew that she hadn't a hope of winning, but everyone else, thinking she was Moonstruck, put their money on her; this meant that he got a very good price on another horse from Codling's stable—Spanish Beach—which would never have beaten the real Moonstruck.

He had pretended to have a row with Mat Codling so that they could use the Eastcombe stables for their dirty work. Also, as pointed out at lunch, by Alex putting up an inexperienced rider the first time, letting him take the blame and then engaging a well-known jockey for the next race, he was given two opportunities for making money.

"Very well thought out," said Alex. "I always knew that Mat was a crafty old bird, but really—. Still in the long run he was no match for you Bradleys."

I blushed but Jon ignored the crack and asked, "Will he lose his licence?"

"Oh, yes, no doubt about that. There'll probably be criminal proceedings as well."

"But what I want to know is *why* did they kidnap *Jimmy*?" asked Katie in a puzzled voice.

"Well, I expect it gave them the fright of their lives, one of our lads prowling round asking for Alan Fane, just when they thought they'd got away with their money-making scheme. They had to keep his mouth shut somehow so I expect they decided to lock him up for a few days while they covered their traces."

"You mean while they were getting rid of the lame grey?" asked Jon.

"No. Of course I can't say for sure," answered Alex, "but my guess is that Sinclair would have picked a quarrel with me, removed his horse, spirited her away to Scotland or somewhere and sold her without a pedigree as an ordinary riding horse. Then the lame filly could have become Moonstruck again, for, even if she doesn't recover enough to race, she'll be a valuable brood mare, whereas our filly wasn't worth her keep."

"But what would they have done with Jimmy?" asked Katie.

"Nothing very terrible. Dumped him miles away in the countryside somewhere and hoped that no one would believe a word he said," answered Alex. "I'm sure that I would have accused him of inventing the whole story to hide the fact that he'd run away."

Later Mark and Jimmy came round to our saddle room and we cleaned tack languidly. Mr Grant's going to take on Alan," Jimmy told us. "Do you know what Codling did? Told Alan he was no good and wrote to his Dad saying he'd never make a stable lad and should try something else, and he'd done two years of his apprenticeship. They wanted him right out of racing, you see, in case he spotted something was wrong."

"What about the lad who did Moonstruck?" asked Jon.

"He was older, a stable lad, not an apprentice, but Alan says he's the sort who'd keep his mouth shut at a price. It'll be nice having Alan here," Jimmy went on, "and better still, Geoff's going."

"Geoff's leaving?" asked Jon.

"Yes," Mark looked remorseful. "I feel bad about it, though he says he wants to go and he is getting too heavy for the flat."

"What's he going to do?" I asked.

"Finish his apprenticeship in a National Hunt stable; Mr Grant's fixed it all up," explained Mark. "He'll be riding over fences, but the horses are full grown, and can carry a bit of weight."

"Well, that's all right then," said Jon.

"Angela will be sad," observed Katie who was polishing a stirrup for me.

"Still, she's going to Art School," I pointed out, "and then all her boy friends will have beards and paint."

"I'd rather they were doctors, then they could tell me stories about accidents," said Katie. "Has Alan broken any bones?"

"His neck, both legs, one arm and cracked his skull," Mark told her and was promptly attacked with a wet sponge. A free fight developed with sponges flying in every direction and no one quite sure which side he was on and then, in the middle of it all, Alex appeared in the doorway.

"I thought somehow," he said, "that these constant tack-cleaning sessions were too good to be true. Now I understand their charm."

"We do clean it," Katie told him, "look at this stirrup, I've been polishing it for ages."

And Jon flapped a leather girth under his nose and asked, "How's that for suppleness?"

Alex ignored them and spoke to Mark. "Sir Richard Orpington, High Jester's owner, has just been on the telephone, he wants you to have the ride on Saturday. All right?"

"Wonderful, thank you very much, sir," answered Mark in official tones, but he looked overjoyed and Jimmy was jumping up and down with delight as though he was eight.

"I thought we might all go racing," Alex looked at me. "Angela says she'll come if Vivien and Jon will, and, of course, we must include Miss Kate."

126

"Oh, I'd love to. On Saturday to watch Mark ride?" I asked.

"Well, there will be other riders to watch, some rather more experienced," mocked Alex.

"A day at the races," said Jon in a contented voice. "That should be good."

"I'm going to put my shirt on High Jester," I announced boldly.

Mark looked rather pleased, but Alex said, "You won't if you take the trainer's advice—a small bet as it's his first time out. I must go back to my telephone," he went on, "the news of a police investigation is spreading fast and I've already had two of Mat Codling's owners making tentative enquiries about sending horses here."

Jon and I looked at each other, both thinking that the Eastcombe luck had changed at last.

Katie said, "If we're going racing on Saturday we *must* settle which day you're taking me for a picnic ride."